BULLET BOOKS
SPEED READS 

ON A PLANE...ON A TRAIN...FASTER THAN A SPEEDING BULLET

SINISTER SANTA

BULLET BOOKS SPEED READS #1

MANNING WOLFE

BILL RODGERS

CONTENTS

Next Book Available   vii

Chapter One   1
Chapter Two   9
Chapter Three   19
Chapter Four   27
Chapter Five   35
Chapter Six   39
Chapter Seven   49
Chapter Eight   57
Chapter Nine   63
Chapter Ten   71
Chapter Eleven   81
Chapter Twelve   93
Chapter Thirteen   99

More Bullet Books   107
Leave a Review   109
Copyright   111

IRON 13

AVAILABLE NOW

TERROR STRIKES . . .

John Hanna is hired by Senator Barry Sands to extricate him from a murderous blackmail scheme designed by terrorist, Fierro. When the Senator's wife is kidnapped, John and Barry find themselves on the trail of the MS-13 terrorist group and discover a sinister plan to assassinate both the American and Russian presidents.

As the clock ticks down can they stop the attack, or will they fall short and witness their worst fears?

CHAPTER ONE

Caldwell Beck eased the rented black Subaru SUV off I-25 and down into Santa Fe, headlights sweeping over the rooftops that sloped with weathered tiles against the dusky horizon. The Sangre de Cristo mountains loomed to the east, their ridges already powdered with white, while the desert behind them stretched flat and endless. A place, Caldwell thought hopefully, where new starts could be found.

Holly shifted beside him, her long scarf tucked into the collar of her coat, body turned toward the window. They hadn't spoken much since they'd flown into Albuquerque. She was still scrolling her phone, thumb moving, as Caldwell looked at the back of her blonde hair.

Downtown came alive as they rolled onto Cerrillos Road and into the Plaza. Adobe storefronts with rounded edges leaned shoulder-to-shoulder, and strings of red chili pepper lights draped across vigas and balconies.

It had been hell getting out of Houston, and they had almost missed their flight. He'd pulled an all-nighter finalizing a motion that had to be filed in order to keep his biggest client from missing a deadline. There had been no choice. The consequences of a late filing would have cost them millions, maybe billions, plus the effect on their stock prices would have been astronomical. He'd wrapped it up that morning and put it in the online cue to go live when the court opened on Monday morning. Of course he'd left instructions for his staff to verify the filing. Nothing would be left to chance.

A light snow began to fall, soft as ash, turning the sidewalks into mottled stone and catching on the shoulders of bundled-up passersby. Street musicians played from under kiva-shaped alcoves, their notes bright in the brittle air.

Holly's departure from Houston hadn't gone much better. She, a journalist and freelance writer, was always on deadline as well. It seemed their whole relationship revolved around one deadline after another, hence the need for the trip. A long, quiet romantic weekend getaway in lovely Santa Fe. Maybe some Christmas shopping for the family. Maybe some time to talk.

Holly hoped they could avoid fighting. Caldwell hoped for some intimate hours in their rental keeping warm under the blankets. It had worked on their prior trips to New Mexico over the years. Maybe the town's special magic would serve them again.

"This town still looks like a Christmas card," Holly said, finally breaking the silence. Her tone was halfway between wonder and fatigue.

Caldwell allowed himself a smile. "That's what I promised, wasn't it? A peaceful respite."

They turned on Agua Fría Street, tires crunching the thin crust of snow, and made several turns through a fairy tale neighborhood. A few minutes later, they pulled into a narrow drive in front of their Airbnb, Casa Pequeno. It was a low adobe house the color of baked clay, with a distinctive flat roof, and featuring a large stucco chimney along the roof line.

Inside, the warmth was immediate, almost startling, the heat having been turned on by housekeeping. The living room opened around a massive corner fireplace, stacked with piñon logs ready to burn. The plaster walls curved softly, painted a muted cream, and the floor was brick, uneven underfoot but glowing from age. A Navajo rug sprawled beneath a heavy oak coffee table, and leather chairs flanked the hearth. The air carried the faint scent of woodsmoke and sage.

Holly dropped her purse on the sofa and circled the room slowly, as though trying to decide if the space felt safe. She admired a Christmas tree that was lit in the corner, adorned with multi-color lights and ornaments crafted from the area. Caldwell watched her remove her jacket, wishing he knew which way her thoughts were running. This trip was supposed to be a fresh start, or at least a pause button, but already the distance between them felt wider than the desert they'd just crossed.

"Pretty tree," she murmured, running a hand along the prickly branches. "Let's see if it helps."

Caldwell returned to the car and came back inside with part of their luggage.

"Did you bring your entire wardrobe?" he laughed.

He had barely dropped their bags inside before Holly said, "We still need to get the rest from the car."

Caldwell tried to joke. "I was hoping you'd forget."

"Not a chance. I'll give you a hand." She thawed a bit as she put her jacket back on over a red sweater she'd bought to try to get into the Christmas spirit. She observed Caldwell and still enjoyed the way he looked, even if she was upset with the way he'd been acting lately.

He was in his mid-thirties, tall and lean, the long muscles of a runner visible under his winter coat. Early mornings pounding miles out along Memorial Park had carved him into shape, his body the only thing he could control in a world where cases spun wild and clients demanded the impossible.

His light-brown hair was slightly overgrown from too many weeks without a trim, swept back with one impatient hand. His face still held the youth of a man not yet weathered by age, but there was a tiredness in his eyes that betrayed long nights at the office and the weight of decisions too big for one set of shoulders.

He wore leather hiking boots, jeans, and a wool sweater under a navy North Face jacket, practical and neat. Weary or not, there was a restless energy to him—an edge sharpened by stress and the constant hum of worry he carried everywhere. Even here, on what was supposed to be a holiday, Caldwell looked like a man fighting to keep his balance, every gesture betraying how much he had worked the past year and all he had riding on this fragile trip.

They stepped back into the cold, their breath visible in the cold air. Caldwell popped the hatch again, reaching for another suitcase. Holly leaned in at the same time and their heads collided.

"Can you not?" she said, jerking back, then pointing at another case in the hatch. "Get your own bag."

"Would you stop micromanaging? I can carry your damn suitcase. Mine, too."

"Last time you said that, you dropped my laptop bag."

"That was one time."

Their voices rose just enough to echo off the adobe walls. From down the street, a large man appeared. He had a long, dark braid down his back and was walking a small dog. Looked like it was part chihuahua. The man slowed, watching the argument unfold.

When Holly glanced his way, the man turned his head sharply, angling his cap low. "Come on, Chico," he spoke to the dog under his breath.

The dog sniffed around, tugging the leash, and relieved himself on a large rock. The man paused but kept his profile hidden.

Caldwell noticed him too and clamped his mouth shut midbickering. Holly followed suit, her words drying up. They each grabbed their own bag without another syllable and shuffled back into the casita.

They went separate ways, investigating the kitchen, bath, and two bedrooms on their own. Both made note of the fact that the second bedroom was set up as an office with a fold out bed inside the sofa. Down the hall, the main bedroom looked small. The king-size bed filled most of the space.

"I'll go pick up the groceries," Caldwell muttered, reaching for the keys again.

Holly didn't look up from the suitcase she was unpacking. "Go ahead. I may take a walk before it gets dark."

"If you're not here, I'll meet you for dinner at the Plaza Cafe. Around seven?"

"Yep."

The snow had thickened when he slid behind the wheel. As he pulled away and headed toward town planning to find Whole Foods curbside, he glanced in the rearview. The door was closed and the porch light was not on.

When he returned, Caldwell pushed open the casita door with his shoulder, both hands straining with brown paper sacks of groceries. The smell of roasted chiles from the Whole Foods parking lot still clung to his clothes.

"Holly?" he called. His voice bounced off the plaster walls. No answer. The air was still.

He carried the bags into the kitchenette, set them on the counter, and methodically pulled out the perishables—milk, eggs, cheese, salad greens—and slid them into the small refrigerator. The motions were automatic, his mind snagging on the silence in the room.

"Holly?" he tried again, louder this time.

Nothing. Something didn't feel right.

He stepped into the bedroom. The bedspread was pulled halfway off the mattress. A pair of shoes lay tipped on their sides as if kicked hard, not set down. Her purse sat on the chair, gaping open, the strap dangling. The nightstand was crowded with Holly's books and magazines. Her engagement ring, left neatly on the wood like punctuation.

He checked the bathroom—towel dropped on the floor, sink still wet from use. Shower dry.

Back in the main room, a throw pillow had slid to the tiles and a chair stood slightly askew. Not chaos, but disturbed, as though she'd been interrupted mid-motion. Maybe she was rushing to get out before he returned.

He pulled his phone from his pocket, tapped her contact from his favorites, and pressed it to his ear. Straight to voicemail.

Caldwell's pulse thudded. The place wasn't trashed, but it wasn't right either. Holly hadn't just walked out, or had she thrown a temper tantrum as she was known to do?

Caldwell left the remaining groceries on the counter and grabbed the keys. He drove to, then parked downtown, one street off the square. He could have walked from the casita, but the temperature was dropping and Holly might prefer to ride home after dinner. He did want to please her, he just didn't know how anymore.

Caldwell entered the Plaza Cafe and scanned the tables and booths. She wasn't there yet. He looked around and chose a booth where he could see the front door and the sidewalk outside through a large picture window.

Caldwell sat with a melting margarita, eyes flicking to the window every thirty seconds. Holly should've been there thirty minutes ago, maybe forty. He checked his watch again, then craned his neck to see up and down the narrow street. Tourists strolled under strings of Christmas lights, couples laughing, kids bundled in puffy jackets, but no Holly.

He stood, went to the counter, and leaned toward the hostess. "Has anyone called here for me? Name's Caldwell."

The young woman shook her head. "No calls for customers tonight."

He returned to the table and waited another thirty minutes. He left a twenty, forced a smile, and walked out, scanning the Plaza one last time before heading down the side street toward the SUV.

CHAPTER TWO

Back at Casa Pequeno, Caldwell quickly changed, tugging on his running clothes as if it were just another evening jog. He tied his running shoes and zipped himself back into his puffy jacket. He could have driven back to the Plaza, but he knew he could cover more ground on foot than in the SUV. He tried to keep his mind steady. She'd gone AWOL before without telling him. Probably found some boutique or gallery that caught her eye. Maybe she'd slipped into another café by mistake. Nothing more. It wasn't facts that disturbed him, it was intuition.

When he stepped into the chill, a light snow fell in lazy flakes dotting his jacket, as he set off at an easy pace. He ran the length of Lincoln through downtown Santa Fe, the air crisp and sharp with the scent of piñon smoke from fireplaces. His breath fogged the air, matching the steam rising from the chimneys overhead.

The Plaza was alive, as always, though thinning out as the night grew darker. Vendors packed away turquoise jewelry and silver bracelets under their blankets while tourists still lingered, snapping photos against the adobe backdrop. Chili pepper lights glowed on strings across shopfronts. Caldwell slowed, scanning faces, peering into shop windows as he passed. No Holly.

He jogged by the Plaza Cafe, but she still hadn't arrived. He turned the corner and opened the door to Starbucks Coffee. She wasn't there either. He told himself not to read too much into it. Holly could be lost in thought, the way she sometimes wandered bookstores for hours, or bent over her phone in some café across town. When she had an idea for a new story or article, she went into a zone where everything was blocked out around her.

He veered into Burro Alley, a narrow cut between tan adobe walls, where lampposts had clicked on. The cobblestones were damp with meltwater, shining under the light. Caldwell checked doorways and recessed arches, half expecting her to step out, brushing her hair back, ready to tease him for being overprotective.

"Probably just mad. Went for a long walk," he murmured. "Or bought out half a store. Please let that be it."

He carried on at a steady jog, covering one side street after another, slipping past galleries with bold canvases in the windows, restaurants already filled with dinner crowds, the clink of silverware carrying out into the street. He made himself wave to a couple walking their dog, as if he weren't searching. As if this were all normal.

Still, his eyes kept darting into every corner, every shaded courtyard, looking for a flash of her coat or the shape of her stride.

So far, nothing.

But Caldwell pressed on, convinced that if he just circled enough blocks, he'd find her.

Caldwell slowed his pace, lungs burning from the thin mountain air. He finally stopped on the corner by St. Francis Basilica, bent at the waist, hands on his knees. Holly wasn't anywhere in the twisting alleys or crowded sidewalks. Not in the Plaza, not in the cafés, not browsing the shops with their adobe walls and ristras hanging bright red in the chill.

He pulled out his phone and called her one more time. "I'm really worried now, Holly. Please call me."

The little blue dot blinked at him, unmoved, steady. He typed Santa Fe Police Department and the address popped up on the screen. He stood still for a moment, heart hammering, reviewed the address, then turned his steps that way.

The streets grew quieter as he jogged past shuttered galleries and dimly-lit restaurants, some closing. His running shoes scuffed the sidewalk in quick, angry bursts. He was trying not to think about what this meant. She was still just mad, or lost, or distracted, wasn't she?

The glass door of the police station reflected him—sweat-slick, winded, not looking much like a lawyer on vacation. He pushed inside. The air smelled faintly of coffee and copier toner.

At the front desk, a uniformed officer raised his eyebrows.

"You need help, sir?"

"Yes. My fiancée's missing. Maybe." The words tumbled out heavier than he expected. "We're staying at a rental. I went to get groceries. When I came back, she was gone. Her purse was there, but the room was off—like someone had been in it."

The officer reached for a pad. "Slow down. Let's get this on record."

Caldwell forced himself to breathe evenly, answering the questions one by one. Name, description, where she'd last been seen. He described the purse on the bed, the chair tilted on its side.

"Do you have a photo?"

Caldwell found one on his phone and handed the phone to the officer who sent it to the police email.

When the report was finalized, the officer said, "We'll put out a notice. You should stay close to your rental in case she turns up."

Caldwell nodded. He wasn't sure he could do that. He wasn't sure of anything anymore, except that Holly was gone and the city around him suddenly felt strange, unfamiliar, like it had turned its face away.

The walk back from the police station felt longer than the run there. Caldwell kept his head on a swivel, looking for her in every corner, replaying the officer's words: *Stay close to your rental in case she turns up.* As if Holly might just stroll back, shopping bags swinging, smile on her lips, and laughing about a misunderstanding.

He arrived at Casa Pequeno, hoping to see the lights on. But when he turned onto their street, the adobe walls glowed with reflections from the streetlights, and the casita looked the same as when he'd left—dark, quiet, too still. Then he saw movement farther down the row of casas. The strange man, now wearing a heavy parka and knit cap, tugged on the leash of the chihuahua. He was leaning against a low stucco wall, pretending to study his phone while the dog sniffed at weeds along the curb.

Caldwell's pulse kicked. He jogged toward him, gravel crunching underfoot.

"Hey!" His voice was sharper than he intended. "You seen

my fiancée? Long blonde hair, red sweater and jeans? She's missing."

Lou Dawg looked up slowly, like someone waking from a dream. His eyes lingered too long, not quite meeting Caldwell's. He gave a thin smile.

"Nope. Haven't seen anyone like that."

Chico whined, shifting its weight, ears back. Lou Dawg jerked the leash a little too hard, then shrugged. "Lots of folks in and out of these rentals. Hard to keep track."

Caldwell felt the hair rise on the back of his neck. The way the man looked at him wasn't sympathy it was watchfulness, like a man assessing him.

"You sure?" Caldwell pressed, stepping closer. "We were right down this way earlier, unloading the SUV. You were walking your dog. You didn't notice her?"

Lou Dawg chuckled without humor, eyes narrowing. "Told you. Haven't seen her."

Caldwell studied him, trying to decide if he was being stonewalled or just dealing with a local crank.

He was a thickset man in his late thirties, with a wrestler's build gone a little soft, his belly pressing against the snap buttons of a worn denim jacket. Long black hair was braided in the style that Indians wore and hung down his back. His broad face carried the blunt features of his Pueblo heritage, but they were hardened by years of what might have been hard living. A crooked scar cut through the stubble on his left cheek, the souvenir of a bar fight he'd never forgotten and often retold.

He smelled to Caldwell faintly of gasoline and smoke. His jeans were frayed, boots caked with red dust. A cigarette smoldered between his fingers, the ember flaring each time he drew on it, then dimming as he exhaled a stream of smoke that curled in the cold night.

The dog tugged again, anxious to move on. Lou Dawg gave

a little nod as if to end the conversation. "Good luck finding her."

Was that sarcasm? Caldwell stood in the cold twilight, watching the man and dog disappear down the street, unease twisting in his gut.

Caldwell unlocked the door of the rental and pushed inside, the weight of the night pressing down on him.

"Holly?" His voice cracked as it filled the little adobe room. Silence answered back.

He moved toward the kitchen. On the counter, the brown paper grocery bags slumped, still half full. A box of crackers, a bunch of bananas, a bag of coffee sat in plain sight, exactly as he'd left them. He remembered putting the milk and cheese into the fridge himself before heading out. Now, the orderliness of the scene made it worse. It looked as if she'd stepped away mid-unpack and never came back, but it was him.

He wandered through the casita, into the bedroom, the bathroom, calling her name each time. The bed was a mess, some clothes tossed on the chair, her purse still sitting there. The ordinary details stabbed at him harder than chaos would have.

He returned to the living room and sank onto the sofa, elbows on knees, hands over his face.

When he could breathe again, he reached for his phone. He called Jared, Holly's brother, first. No answer. Straight to voice-mail. He tried Holly's mother, and she picked up on the fourth ring.

"No, I haven't heard from her. She didn't call; she didn't text. Caldwell, what's happening?" Her voice sharpened with panic.

Reluctant to alarm her as her age and health had been

issues recently, he calmed his voice, but the words felt like lead in his mouth. "We had a spat. I'm sure she'll return shortly. If she calls you, will you let me know right away?"

"Of course." They rang off.

Next, he called Monica, Holly's sister. Same questions and answers as Monica became more alarmed.

"The police know. I filed a report, but no one knows where she is."

Her sister gasped. "Gone? What do you mean gone?"

"I mean she vanished." He squeezed his eyes shut. "I went out to the store. When I came back, she wasn't here."

"Find her. Please. Just find her."

"I'm trying," he whispered, before ending the call. His chest tightened until he almost broke down. He felt the tears behind his eyes, fear mixing with exhaustion.

For the next hour, he sat on the sofa dialing every number he could think of. Friends back in Houston, a couple of her colleagues, even people she hadn't spoken to in months. No one had seen her, no one had heard from her. Each "no" tightened the vise inside his chest.

At last, the phone lay heavy on the coffee table, screen dimming to black. He had to do something.

He called Holly's number again and heard it ringing in the bedroom. He ran in and listened until he located it under the bed.

"Under the bed? How?" She would never leave without her phone.

He took the phone to the living room and immediately called the police and updated the report with the information about the phone. Still no word on their end.

"Please let me know right away if anything turns up."

Caldwell leaned back into the sofa, staring at the ceiling beams. He replayed every moment since they'd arrived—

unloading the car, ordering the groceries online, the strained silences, the way she'd looked at him when their heads had collided over the luggage.

The silence of the casita deepened. His body sagged into the cushions, worn down by fear, the all-nighter at work, and the high desert altitude while running. He told himself he'd just close his eyes for a minute, just rest until his thoughts became clearer. She would surely call.

Sleep crept in slow and heavy, pulling him under.

Two hours later, a sharp crash outside jolted him upright. His heart slammed against his ribs. The room was dark, shadows stretching across the walls from the bathroom light, the faint orange glow of a streetlamp leaking through the curtains.

Then more sounds—scrape, shuffle, like footsteps on gravel just outside the window.

Caldwell held his breath and strained to listen. Someone was out there and they weren't being particularly quiet about it.

Holly?

Caldwell eased off the sofa, his shoes still on from the run to the police station. Every sound in the casita seemed magnified —the creak of the floorboards, the heat from the vents. He reached for his phone, but the battery icon blinked red, nearly drained.

The scrape came again, closer now, followed by a low thump against the wall.

He moved to the window, lifted the curtain just enough to peer through. The streetlamp cast a pale-orange circle onto the driveway, but most of the yard lay in shadow. He saw the outline of something, or someone, shift near the woodpile stacked along the side of the neighboring casa.

Caldwell swallowed hard, then turned the deadbolt and stepped outside. The cold night air slapped his face, sharp with the scent of juniper and thin mountain air. He tightened his fists and cleared his throat.

"Who's there?" His voice cracked the silence. "Holly?"

A pause. Then the sound of gravel crunching as a figure straightened from the shadows.

The man stepped into the dim halo of the streetlamp—a bulky frame in a hooded parka, cigarette glowing faintly. Caldwell could make out the loop of a leash hanging from one hand.

"We didn't introduce ourselves earlier," the man said, his voice low and raspy. "Name's Lou Dawg. You're the lawyer."

Caldwell felt his pulse thump. Was it a question or a declaration? "Yeah. Caldwell." He hesitated, every instinct telling him not to move closer. "Out here late?"

Lou Dawg shrugged, the cigarette tip flaring. "Walking the dog. Same as always."

Caldwell scanned the street. "Don't see a dog."

"Likes the shadows," Lou Dawg said with a grin that didn't reach his eyes. "You yelling for somebody?"

"My fiancée," Caldwell said, his tone sharper now. "I still haven't located her."

Lou Dawg took a slow drag, then exhaled smoke into the cold air. "That so? Shame." He didn't look surprised.

"You still haven't seen her?" Caldwell pressed.

Lou Dawg gave another shrug. "Lots of folks coming and going. Can't say I keep track."

Chico barked suddenly from behind the low stucco wall, startling them both. Lou Dawg gave a whistle and the barking stopped.

He flicked the cigarette into the gravel and ground it under his boot. "Better get some rest, Caldwell. Long day. Longer night ahead if you're out here askin' strangers questions."

Without waiting for a response, Lou Dawg and Chico melted into the darkness, footsteps and dog's nails clicking against stone.

Caldwell stood frozen, shoes planted on cold gravel, watching him vanish. A chill worked its way down his spine. It was as if Lou Dawg wanted him to know he was being watched.

"And, how does he know I'm a lawyer?"

CHAPTER THREE

Caldwell went inside and plugged in his phone. He sat on the sofa and waited for enough juice to start calling again. Hours later, he woke stiff on the sofa, the gray light of dawn filtering through the curtains. His head throbbed from too little sleep and too much dread. For a long moment, he lay still, listening, half expecting to hear Holly call his name from the bedroom. But the casita was silent.

He sat up, rubbed his face, and reached for his phone. He called the police, but they had nothing. His calls to friends and family the night before had gone nowhere. He needed a new angle.

His eyes landed on the small placard by the door—the laminated sheet with the Wi-Fi info and local emergency numbers. At the bottom was the number for the rental company.

He dialed, pacing the room until a chipper voice came on the line. "Adobe Casitas Management, this is Teresa. How may I help you?"

"This is Caldwell Beck. I'm renting Casa Pequeno, unit four, off Agua Fría. My fiancée is missing. I filed a police report last night. I need to know, does this property have cameras?"

There was a pause, the woman's tone shifting. "I'm so sorry. Yes, sir. There's a Ring doorbell camera on that unit. It shoots video."

"Can you check it? Please. Timeframe between about five and seven last night." His voice cracked, raw from the night.

"Hold on." He could hear typing, muffled voices. Minutes stretched like hours. Finally, she came back, voice hushed. "There's something here. I'll describe it. A large man in a ballcap pulled low so his face isn't clear. He's escorting a woman out the door. Petite. Blonde hair. She looks... reluctant. He's got her by the arm."

Caldwell's knees buckled, and he sank onto the sofa. "That's her. That's Holly. Can you text that to me?"

"I don't know. I'll have to check with the manager."

"No, don't waste time. Just send it to the police."

"Yes, sir. We'll share this with the police immediately."

"Wait," Caldwell said, desperate. "The man. Anything about him? His build, clothes?"

She hesitated. "Medium height, heavy jacket. A braid down his back. Part of a dog shows up in the frame, briefly. Could be a terrier or another small breed."

Caldwell's pulse pounded. "The braid, the dog." His mind snapped to the cigarette glow, the leash dangling from a thick hand. Lou Dawg.

"It must be him." he whispered to himself, barely audible.

"Sir?" Teresa asked.

"Nothing. Just send that video to the police."

"Of course. Right away."

Caldwell hung up, phone slippery in his grip. He leaned forward, elbows on his knees, the image burning in his mind:

Holly being dragged out the very door he was staring at. The man's cap pulled low, the dog at his side.

Lou Dawg. It had to be. He looked out the picture window at the street. No one was out in the cold morning air. He bundled up, grabbed his keys, and ran out. He jumped in the SUV and retraced his path from the night before to the police station.

The Santa Fe Police Department looked different in the daylight, but Caldwell felt no calmer as he pushed through the glass doors. He was disheveled from sleeping on the sofa, his jaw tight with fatigue. He walked straight to the front desk.

"I'm Caldwell Beck. I filed a missing persons report last night. Holly, my fiancée."

The uniformed officer behind the counter glanced at his computer, then motioned him toward a small interview room. A detective in plain clothes joined them.

"I'm Detective Sampson. I'll be handling your missing persons case."

Caldwell nodded.

Detective Ray Sampson had the kind of presence that filled a room without raising his voice. Mid-fifties, broad-shouldered, his frame carried the weight of a man who'd spent years kicking down doors and now wore the experience like armor. His hair was more silver than black, clipped close at the sides, with deep lines cut across his forehead from decades of squinting against both desert sun and human deceit.

He wore a suit of muted colors—grays and tans that blended with the adobe walls of the city outside—but his bolo tie and scuffed cowboy boots gave away his New Mexico roots.

His badge was tucked in a leather case on his belt, more practical than showy.

As Caldwell observed him, Sampson spoke in a slow, measured cadence, a dry edge of Santa Fe gravel in his voice, the kind of tone that made suspects talk too much and victims finally breathe. Locals respected him because he'd grown up just outside the city, in Española, and never forgot where he came from. He understood the push and pull between the police and the tribal lands, between the city's glittering tourism and the poverty hidden in the arroyos. That knowledge made him cautious, but it also made him fair. He studied Caldwell with a discerning eye.

"We've already received security footage from your house rental company. Shows a man escorting your fiancée out the door. Ballcap pulled low, maybe a dog at his side. Looks like she wasn't going willingly. She wasn't wearing a coat. No purse."

"May I see it?"

Sampson nodded at the officer who cued it up on a laptop for Caldwell to see.

Caldwell's throat tightened. "That's her. That's Holly." He leaned forward. "That man could be the man called Lou Dawg. He's been hanging around our street, always outside, always watching. Last night, I confronted him right outside our casita. Somehow he knows I'm a lawyer."

The detective frowned. "Could this be a robbery or a kidnapping for ransom?"

"No way. Her engagement ring was on the nightstand where she left it. Her purse was there, too."

"Why wasn't she wearing her engagement ring?"

"We were fighting, okay?" Caldwell snapped. "But you've got a man on video taking her out of my rental and you're asking me if we had a spat?" His voice echoed in the small room, and the detective's jaw hardened.

"Sir, calm down. I'm not insinuating anything."

"No, I won't calm down. Why didn't you get the footage from the rental company yourselves? Why did it take *me* calling them? You're moving too slow, and my fiancée—she could be —" His voice cracked. He slammed his palm against the table. "She could be gone for good if you don't act."

The room went still. Caldwell realized he'd crossed a line. He needed their help.

The detective's eyes narrowed. "We *are* acting. You want us to take this seriously? Then you give us everything. Starting with the truth. Did you have anything to do with this?"

Caldwell swallowed hard. His pride said no, but the weight of it dragged the words out anyway. "Yes. We were fighting. We came here trying to patch things up, but it didn't go well. She took off her ring. We argued. But I swear to you, I had nothing to do with this. I went to the store, and when I came back, she was gone. She was supposed to meet me for dinner, but she never showed."

"Anything else?"

"This Lou Dawg character was hanging around outside all day and night. He introduced himself, but it wasn't natural. It was like a warning or something."

Detective Sampson studied him for a long moment, then nodded slowly. "That matters. Now we know where you stand. You admit there was conflict, you admit you left."

Caldwell sagged against the chair, exhaustion washing over him. "So, what happens now?"

The detective's tone softened just a notch. "We already put out a missing persons notice last night. If this Lou Dawg is connected, we'll find out. But you need to stay out of the way. Go back to your rental and stay put. If he comes sniffing around again, you call us. Do not try to handle him yourself."

Caldwell nodded reluctantly, though inside fire burned

hotter than ever. He didn't trust them to move fast enough. And he wasn't sure he could just sit and wait.

Caldwell drove back along Agua Fría, the detective's words still ringing in his ears: *Stay out of the way*. He couldn't. Not while Holly was out there.

The casita looked the same as when he'd left it—quiet, empty, too still. He parked and got out of the SUV, paused at the entrance, then turned down the street instead. His gaze locked on the low-walled casa where Lou Dawg had slunk back to the night before.

He marched up to the first door, eyes squinting in the sun, and knocked. A woman in a brightly colored housecoat cracked it open, a wary eye peering past the chain. Caldwell could see the twinkling lights of a Christmas tree behind her. *Here Comes Santa Cause* was playing from somewhere inside the house.

"Sorry to bother you," Caldwell said quickly. "I'm looking for a man—burly, wears a parka, ballcap, walks a little chihuahua mix. Calls himself Lou Dawg. You know him?"

The woman shook her head. "Not from this street."

"But he came to this house."

"Not my house." She closed the door with finality.

Caldwell moved on, knocking at another. A middle-aged man in paint-streaked jeans leaned against the frame, wiping his hands on a rag. "Lou Dawg? Never heard of him. We know most of the folks here. He doesn't live on this block."

At the third house, a younger woman with a toddler on her hip frowned at the description. "Small dog, you say? No, we don't see him around here. Not like that. Whoever he is, he no live here."

Each answer stoked the fire in Caldwell's gut. Lou Dawg

wasn't just a shady neighbor—he wasn't a neighbor at all. He had no reason to be hanging around the casitas, except one.

By the time Caldwell circled back to his own door, his chest was tight, his pulse hammering. He was turning the lock when his phone buzzed in his pocket.

He yanked it out, fumbled with the screen, then ran inside to answer, the door slamming shut behind him. An unknown number.

"Hello?" His voice was hoarse.

There was a beat of silence on the line, then a low voice came through.

"You should stop looking, Caldwell. She's long gone. You'll never find her unless you do what I say." The pause was long and ominous.

His grip tightened on the phone, breath sharp in his throat. He forced the words out, steady despite the fear rising inside him.

"What do you want?"

CHAPTER FOUR

Caldwell gripped the phone tighter, every muscle in his body coiled. "Who are you?"

The voice on the other end was low and mocking. "Just call me Santa."

Caldwell's stomach lurched. "Santa? What the hell do you want with my fiancée?"

Santa chuckled, a dry rasp. "What I want is simple. You'll do a few things for my client, and when I'm satisfied, Holly will walk free. Until then, she stays with Lou Dawg. You know, the guy you met outside last night."

The words dropped like stones into Caldwell's gut. He tried to steady his breathing, to keep control. "You expect me to take your word for it? Put her on the phone. I need to know she's alive."

"You'll get a call from Lou Dawg in five minutes." The line went dead.

When the phone rang a few minutes later, Caldwell answered after the first ring. There was a muffled scuffle, then a woman's voice broke through—thin, urgent. "Caldwell? It's me—"

"Holly!"

"Listen—" Her voice dropped to a hurried whisper. "I'm okay. I love you."

"I love you. Have they hurt you?"

"No. Tripping on the blue glass."

A grunt, then the line jolted as the phone was ripped away.

"Enough," Lou Dawg snapped. "You'll get instructions soon. Follow them exactly, or she won't be calling you again."

The line went dead.

Caldwell stared at the phone, heart hammering. Her voice replayed in his head—desperate, deliberate. Tripping? Blue glass? What had she meant? A landmark? A building? What could they possibly want from him? He didn't have millions. He wasn't a powerful man. He was just an average lawyer.

He paced the casita, running the phrase over and over. Blue glass. He couldn't make sense of it. Not yet.

He pressed the phone to his forehead, eyes shut tight. Somewhere out there, Holly was trying to reach him. Trying to tell him where she was. And he'd missed it.

No one in Houston's legal or business circles knew Santa's real name. To most, he was the Fixer, a whispered threat in boardrooms and backrooms alike. But to the men who signed the checks at GulfTex, he was George Saint. Santa was a mocking nickname he'd once embraced because it reminded him of the way he delivered: always what the client wanted, never what was deserved.

Saint, or Santa, had worked for GulfTex for over twenty years, though his connection to power went back further. He wasn't on the payroll in any official sense. There were no bene-fits, no pension, no HR file tucked in a cabinet. He was a contractor of shadows, hired again and again when the oil giant needed things done outside the lines of law and ethics. Landowners refusing to sell? Santa had ways of convincing them. Regulators nosing around too closely? Santa found lever-age. Sometimes it was a vice, sometimes a family secret, always a threat too sharp to ignore.

His background was as fractured and brutal as the work he did. Born in East Texas, raised in a house where whiskey was cheaper than bread, he'd joined the Army at seventeen, a natural brawler who found purpose in violence. Military training honed him, gave him the discipline his childhood lacked. He learned how to disappear, how to make others disappear, how to bend fear into a weapon. When he left the service, he didn't fit into civilian life, but GulfTex saw a use for a man like him. They plucked him out of obscurity after he roughed up a union organizer in Port Arthur at the direction of a small-time drilling company. From then on, he belonged to them.

Saint was ruthless because he believed in results, not reasons. He had no patience for excuses or moral debates. Once, in Midland, he'd burned down a man's barn while his cattle still slept inside, all because the man refused to sign over mineral rights. Another time, in Corpus Christi, he left a company rival bloodied in a parking lot with a whispered reminder: Stay out of GulfTex territory. These weren't stories people told openly, but the fear lingered. Everyone in the oil patch knew Santa was out there, and everyone knew he'd never been caught.

He enjoyed the work in his own way. Not for the money, though GulfTex paid him enough to live any way or anywhere he pleased. It was the control. Watching people squirm, watching good men break when the pressure got tight enough. It was an art form to him, more satisfying than any painting or sculpture. Fear was his medium and he applied it with precision.

Lou Dawg had been one of his finds, a wild kid from the reservation with a mean streak and a willingness to follow orders. Santa saw potential in him, shaped him into muscle that could be trusted. Where Santa dealt in strategy and menace, Lou Dawg was the blunt instrument, a loyal hound who never asked why.

Now, with Holly Rowe locked away and Caldwell Beck dancing on the end of the line, Santa felt the familiar thrill of a game already half won. GulfTex had called, and as always, he delivered. The lawyer thought he was clever, thought he could pace his little casita floorboards and puzzle out a path to save her. Santa almost laughed at the thought. Men like Beck, men with reputations to protect, were the easiest to crack. Fear of losing everything did half the work.

Santa sat in the dark of his safe house just outside Santa Fe, phone on the table, letting Caldwell Beck sweat it out. His eyes were flat, predatory, untroubled by what might come next. Holly was leverage. Lou Dawg was muscle. Caldwell was prey. And GulfTex, as always, was the hand that fed him.

He called Lou Dawg at his trailer on the reservation and asked how things were going.

"Great. She's in the bedroom. Still out from the drugs I gave her after the call to the lawyer. Should sleep for hours."

Caldwell paced the tile around the casita. The phone rang again less than an hour later. Caldwell snatched it up before the first buzz finished.

"Santa?" His voice was raw.

"You wanted proof of life, you got it," the voice said coolly. "Now it's time you earn it."

Caldwell clenched his jaw. "What do you want from me?"

"You're an attorney. That makes you useful." Santa's tone carried a sneer. "Back in Houston, you've got a case, *Johnson v. GulfTex Holdings*. Big stakes. Big motion pending. Due to be filed electronically before the Court opened on before Monday morning."

Caldwell's pulse jumped. He'd been working on it for months. It was the motion he'd completed when they left for Santa Fe. "What about it?"

"You're going to kill it. Log in to your court's filing portal and sabotage the motion."

"I've already set it up to be filed first thing Monday morning. It's too late."

"It's not filed yet. You can withdraw it or change it. Doesn't matter how, just so long as it blows up in your client's face."

"That case is important to my client," Caldwell said. "If I do what you're asking, I could lose my license. My career."

"You'll lose more than that if you don't," Santa cut in sharply. "She dies. Simple math."

Caldwell swallowed hard, fighting to keep his voice level. "Why me? Why that case?"

"You don't get to ask questions. What matters is the deadline. If I see a filing confirmation before the deadline expires, you'll be digging a grave instead of planning your next cross-examination."

Caldwell said, forcing the words out, "How will you know?"

"We'll be monitoring the court's docket online. I'll know."

Caldwell's hand tightened around the phone.

There was silence on the line.

For a split second, Holly's face appeared before him. Caldwell stood frozen, the phone pressed to his ear, his breath jagged.

Santa grunted. "If you go to the police again or call anyone, we'll know. We're watching and listening. You make one false move and she's gone." The line went dead.

Caldwell sank onto the sofa, head in his hands. *Sabotage the motion, destroy my client, destroy myself, or lose her.*

His watch read 9:17 a.m. That gave him just under forty-eight hours. Time to think. Time to search. Time to stall. Time to figure out the blue glass.

Caldwell sat on the edge of the bed, his phone heavy in his hand. The kidnappers had warned him: *Do as we say. Don't call anyone.*

He could go to the police again, but what if that asshole was outside watching him? Maybe they weren't tracking the phone at the rental. He went to the kitchen without turning on the lights. He looked at the phone on the wall.

Could they know about the wall phone? Most places don't have land lines anymore. What are the odds?

It was a risk, but he couldn't sit in silence any longer. He punched in the main number for his Houston office.

"Jeffries Ortega & Beck," the receptionist chirped. "How may I direct your call?"

"This is Caldwell Beck. Put me through to Paul Jeffries."

"I'm sorry, Mr. Beck, Mr. Jeffries has left for the day."

"Try Robert Dwyer."

"Yes, sir. One moment."

Clicks on the line, then a pause long enough for doubt to claw at him. Caldwell rubbed his temple, bracing himself.

Dwyer had been his associate for over two years. He was young, but he would be able to track down a partner, figure it out.

When the call finally connected, the voice that came through wasn't warm, or even surprised. It was controlled. Cold.

"Caldwell," Dwyer said. "You shouldn't have called."

Caldwell froze. "Bob? What the hell are you talking about? I need help. It's the GulfTex case. Holly's gone. They took her."

There was no sharp intake of breath. No rush of concern. Just silence stretching thin as wire. Then, finally, Dwyer spoke, quiet and deliberate.

"How do you think they knew you were in Santa Fe? How do you think they're monitoring the online filing portal?"

The words hit harder than a fist. Caldwell's chest tightened. He stumbled to his feet, pacing the small kitchen, gripping the phone so tightly it cut into his palm. "You?" His voice cracked into a growl. "You little bastard. You sold me out."

"It's only business. Pull the motion like they told you and maybe she lives. But don't call here again. The partners don't know and I suggest you keep it that way. Next time, it won't just be a warning."

"Dwyer." Caldwell's voice rose, raw, shaking with fury and fear. "I swear to God."

The line went dead.

Caldwell stood there, staring at the phone, his pulse roaring in his ears. A man he'd mentored, trained, brought along case by case. The betrayal hollowed him out. He lowered the phone slowly, his hand trembling, every nerve screaming.

His associate. His right hand. The rot had been inside the house all along.

CHAPTER FIVE

aldwell sat on the edge of the couch again, elbows on his knees. The call still echoed in his mind. Santa's gravelly voice, calm but deadly clear: *Withdraw the Motion for Summary Judgment or she disappears forever.* Dwyer's betrayal cut him off from his partners.

Could he do it? Against every instinct as a lawyer, every obligation to his client, he had logged in and was staring at the court docket. He had to protect Holly over his client. But maybe there was another way to save them both.

He was on his own. His law firm couldn't help. He dared not call the client. He couldn't go to the police. He could think of nothing.

The room was too quiet, every creak of the old adobe house amplifying the hollow thud of his pulse. He rubbed his face with both hands. What if pulling the motion wasn't enough? What if they never meant to return her?

He heard footsteps outside, then the sharp ring of the doorbell jolted him upright.

Caldwell's chest tightened as he stood. He crossed to the door and eased it open.

No one was there. Only a cardboard box, small, unmarked, sitting on the door mat.

He stepped out onto the porch and looked up and down the street. He saw no one.

He picked up the package and carried it inside. Setting it on the table, he opened the lid with shaky hands.

Inside a folded square of tissue paper was a lock of Holly's blonde hair, bound with twine.

His stomach knotted, rage and fear twisting together. A slip of paper sat beside it. He unfolded it.

If you doubt us, this is proof. Next time you make a call, it will be a toe or a finger. Do exactly as you're told.

It was signed at the bottom, in thick, jagged scrawl:

Ho Ho Ho, Santa.

Caldwell let the note fall to the table. He stared at the lock of hair until his vision blurred, fists clenched. If he could have reached Bob Dwyer in that moment, he would have strangled him.

They were proving their point. They would harm her. He knew, with chilling certainty, that this wasn't a game and it was just the beginning.

Caldwell sat down at the table, the box with Holly's hair pushed to one side. His laptop glowed in the dim light, the court's online docket still open like a judge staring him down.

He swallowed hard, his throat dry, and guided the cursor to the case file: *Johnson v. GulfTex Holdings.* Caldwell had represented Louis Johnson for almost his entire legal career. How could he possibly betray him?

There it was, the Motion to Dismiss, the centerpiece of his defense, the one thing standing between GulfTex and a billion-dollar payday at his client's expense. The deadline was Monday. If the motion disappeared, so did Louis Johnson's chance to argue his motion to dismiss. Of course, a judge could allow an extension, but Caldwell had never seen one. And, what if they kept Holly until after the hearing on the motion? She could be missing for days while he was back in Houston in court, far away from her and unable to do anything.

Caldwell's hand hovered over the trackpad. His mind filled with images of Holly—her laugh over dinner, the way she always tapped his arm when she got excited, her head on his shoulder in the quiet after long days. He could almost hear her voice telling him not to give in. But then he saw the box again, the lock of her hair, and Santa's taunting scrawl: *Next time, a toe or a finger.*

His stomach turned. He clicked.

The system asked for confirmation. *Withdraw Motion?*

He sat frozen, then forced his fingers to move. *Yes.*

The screen blinked, and just like that, the Motion to Dismiss was gone. Since it had never been filed, not a trace was left. Only the draft in the firm portal. Impotent.

Caldwell pressed his palms against his eyes, the weight of what he'd done crashing down on him. Without that motion, Johnson would be steamrolled. GulfTex would take the case all the way to the Supreme Court if they had to. They'd never give up, and they'd cheat to win. They'd delay and delay, all the while drilling on his land.

On Monday morning, the deadline would pass. Johnson's case would collapse. And Caldwell would take the fall. He could already see the malpractice suits piling up, his partners disappointed in him, the Bar Association coming for his license. His firm would not survive this.

And most likely, neither.

He dropped his hands and stared at the empty docket, his reflection faint on the screen. He had just betrayed his client, his oath, and his career, all for Holly.

He whispered into the silence, "God help me, this better be enough to bring her back."

CHAPTER SIX

Caldwell Beck had spent more than a decade in Houston courtrooms, the kind where billion-dollar oil and gas companies went to war over leases, royalties, and contracts that could stretch longer than their pipelines. He wasn't the flashiest lawyer in town, nor the richest, but his reputation carried weight. Judges knew him as steady. Juries trusted him. Even opposing counsel sometimes admitted, off the record, that Beck played hard but fair.

He'd made partner early at a mid-size downtown firm, the kind with brushed-steel nameplates in the lobby and oil derrick art on the walls. His first big break had come when he defended a small family-run drilling outfit against a conglomerate that tried to assert rights they didn't have. Against the odds, Beck found the clause no one else had discovered and turned the case around. The family still sent him Christmas cards, a reminder that the law could still be about people, not just companies.

Over the years, he'd tried cases in federal and state courts, argued before the Fifth Circuit, and published a couple of articles in respected law reviews. The Texas Bar had given him a nod with its "Top Litigator Under Forty" recognition, but Beck didn't hang plaques all over his office. He'd always figured his work spoke loud enough. When one of the named partners passed on, the other two remaining promoted him. Now his name was on the wall with theirs: *Jeffries Ortega & Beck.*

What mattered most was how he carried himself. He treated his staff like associates, not servants. He answered his own phone more often than his assistant liked. And when young lawyers asked him how to build a career, he told them the truth: Listen first. Clients don't hire you to talk. They hire you to solve problems.

He wasn't perfect, especially when it came to relationships. Too many late nights, too much caffeine, not enough time for dating, but in the cutthroat world of Houston litigation, Caldwell Beck still believed in something old-fashioned: being the kind of lawyer you could trust.

Now, staring at the impossible demand Santa and Lou Dawg had placed on him, he felt the weight of that trust like a stone on his chest. If he bent the rules, even once, every verdict, every handshake, every Christmas card from grateful clients would crumble into dust. His reputation had taken a lifetime to build and would take only a moment to ruin. Worse, he wondered if he could ever look at himself in the mirror again.

Caldwell paced the length of the casita, the beams above his head looming like crossbars on a cage. His mind churned on the two questions that mattered: *Where is Holly? What blue glass?*

Of all the cases he'd handled, why had Santa latched on to this one?

Louis Johnson wasn't just any client. He was a rancher from Lubbock, a stubborn man with weathered skin and a slow drawl who had decided to take on one of the biggest oil and gas outfits in Texas. GulfTex Holdings had been drilling on Johnson's land for years under a lease drawn up in the 1970s. Back then, oil was king and the contracts were written to favor the companies.

But things had changed. Horizontal drilling and hydraulic fracturing had opened up new reservoirs beneath Johnson's property. There were minerals worth millions. GulfTex claimed the old lease gave them the right to extract it all. Johnson insisted the lease had limitations and that the company was overreaching. He felt he had a good case for a motion for summary judgment and had drawn a favorable judge who listened to the facts and relied on the four corners of the lease document.

The motion Caldwell had prepared, the motion he was ordered to sabotage, was the heart of the case: a motion for summary judgment that would decide whether GulfTex had a legal right to drill more on the same land. If Caldwell won, Johnson would have control over the remainder of his unleased land and the mineral rights beneath it. If he lost, GulfTex would start a new drilling program under the old lease.

Santa's demand made a cruel kind of sense. Sabotage the filing by withdrawing it entirely and Johnson's case would take a major blow. The case would then go to trial where GulfTex might actually convince a jury to side with them. Millions of dollars in future oil and gas revenue would most likely slide into GulfTex's pocket. If nothing else, the delay would give them time to expand their drilling program.

Caldwell stopped at the window, looking out into the dusky street where the lamplight pooled faint and weak. He rubbed the back of his neck, feeling the weight of it press harder.

Sabotage meant betraying Johnson, a man who'd put his trust in him, who had told him more than once: *You're the only lawyer I've ever met who looks me in the eye.*

But if he didn't... Holly.

Caldwell pressed his palms against the cold glass and shut his eyes. GulfTex was ruthless—he knew that. They'd burned through smaller landowners like brush fires, leaving them penniless and dispossessed. They had an army of lawyers on retainer, a full-time PR firm to scrub their image, and the deep pockets to keep fighting for years. They just had to get past this initial motion for summary judgment. When that happened, the case would go to trial and they could milk Johnson dry with filings, legal fees, and delays.

He turned away from the window and dropped back onto the sofa, head in his hands. The clock on the wall ticked loud in the silence. He had thirty-six hours to choose between his client's future and Holly's life.

He could go online and change the filing back to active. Maybe he could think of a way around Santa and Lou Dawg. He needed help. How could he reach out to his partners without being seen or possibly get word to the police or the court in Houston?

He looked around the room as if searching for help. Then he remembered Holly's phone. He'd fished it out from under the bed when he'd found her missing. He went into the bedroom and snatched it off the nightstand. Her engagement ring still sat there, a reminder of their bickering and harsh words that meant so little now.

He went back in the living room and placed her phone on the coffee table, staring at it and wondering if they were monitoring it as well. Why would they? They had her and they might not have considered keeping tabs on her phone. But what if they had someone else on the inside like Bob Dwyer? If they could get to him, they could get to anyone.

The phone sat on the coffee table, screen black, small and silent, but alive in its own way. Caldwell continued to stare at it like it might bite, unable to decide whether it was salvation or a trap.

If he picked it up, he could call the one group of people who might actually be able to help—his partners back in Houston. Names ran through his mind like cards shuffled in a deck. Paul Jeffries, senior partner, hard-nosed but loyal, the one who had vouched for him when he made partner. Dana Ortega, brilliant strategist, the best he'd ever seen in a courtroom, someone who would listen before asking why he sounded like a lunatic on a borrowed phone. Either of them would move mountains if he asked. But the warning echoed in his head: Santa and Lou Dawg had said they were monitoring his phone, his texts. They hadn't mentioned Holly's phone. Still, would they be stupid enough to leave a door like that unguarded?

GulfTex wasn't just a company, it was an empire. They had the money to buy entire teams of hackers who could ghost through phone lines, pull call logs, and sift e-mails in real time. For all he knew, someone was already watching, waiting for him to slip, for one panicked call to light up a screen in some dark surveillance room.

Caldwell rubbed his temples, eyes fixed on the phone's dark reflection of the casita ceiling. He imagined making the call, then he imagined the fallout: a knock at the door, or worse, another package delivered with the promise of her finger or toe.

He thought of other options. He could find a payphone, if such a thing even existed in Santa Fe anymore, but they said they were watching him. He could sneak out a window and jog down to the police station, but that would be the first place they would monitor. Every path circled back to the same dead end: risk.

Holly's phone vibrated suddenly with a reminder, just a calendar alert of a dinner reservation at The Shed, but the sound made him flinch. He turned it facedown, the weight of it pressing onto the table as if it wanted him to choose.

For now, he didn't. He slid the phone toward him and tucked it into his jacket pocket. A lifeline, maybe. Or a fuse. He would hold it close, bide his time, and hope that he could come up with a better plan before time ran out.

Lou Dawg, a member of the Kewa Santo Domingo Pueblo Tribe, had been causing trouble his whole life. He lived in a mobile home, a single-wide two-bedroom on the Cochiti Reservation about an hour southwest of Santa Fe, where he kept a low profile. He had intentionally chosen a trailer site off a gravel road that didn't connect to anything else on the reservation. One way in and one way out.

He could have afforded a newer pickup, but he held on to his old, beat-up Ford and a secondhand tractor rigged for mowing the scruff on the patch of land around his trailer. He called no unnecessary attention to himself as he banked his earnings for the day when he'd leave the reservation for good.

He'd grown up on the reservation adoring his mother, who wove coiled yucca baskets and supplied them to a small art gallery in town that catered to tourists. The work was slow and the volume low, but the quality was high. She wove intricate patterns that sold for good money when the right buyer came along. His father was a different story. He had the devil of alcohol in his blood and drank up most of the profits from the basket sales.

Lou Dawg had considered his mother a saint before her death a few years back. His father, by contrast, was evil incarnate. The booze made him a mean drunk, and he had no interest in changing his nasty ways. Lou Dawg tolerated him for his mother's sake, but after her death, his patience snapped. During one of their many fights, he shoved his father hard. The man fell, cracked his head on a rock, and never got up again. Tribal Police called it an accident, filed the paperwork, and moved on. Maybe Lou Dawg had pushed him too hard on purpose, maybe not. Either way, no one asked questions.

Lou Dawg didn't work steady, picking up small jobs when someone needed a private investigator, a lookout, or a bit of petty theft done without fingerprints. Recently, he'd been hired to get rid of a fancy SUV he figured had been used in Albuquerque for a smash-and-grab job at a jewelry store. He couldn't prove it, but after catching the news reports, he'd put two and two together.

This was his third job for Santa, but his first kidnapping. So far, it had gone smoother than he'd imagined. He'd snatched the girl at the casita when her boyfriend left her to unpack, hustled her out the door and into his truck without a soul noticing.

She was asleep now, knocked out from the drugs he'd slipped her, tied and gagged in the second bedroom of the trailer. If she happened to wake up, she wasn't going anywhere. That freed him to head back up to Santa Fe and keep eyes on Caldwell Beck for Santa.

Lou Dawg sat in his truck at the end of the street, parked where a makeshift fence of aspen poles lashed together with vines and twine gave him cover as he watched Caldwell's rental. The cold air fogged his windshield and he leaned forward, squinting through the haze before kicking up the defroster. The heater coughed, spitting a mix of dust and stale heat. A cigarette glowed between his fingers, the ember pulsing like a watchful eye.

From this angle, he had a clean sightline to the casita's front door and picture window. Warm light spilled through, shadows stretching across the adobe walls. Inside, Caldwell paced like a trapped animal, hands shoved into his pockets, jaw tight, a man fighting his own thoughts. Lou Dawg watched, patient and steady; Chico curled on the torn vinyl seat beside him, the dog's shallow breaths fogging a tiny patch of glass.

Lou Dawg drummed his free hand against the steering wheel. He had learned long ago that surveillance wasn't about adrenaline or drama; it was about waiting, about letting the silence press in until the other guy cracked. Caldwell hadn't called the police, not yet. If he had, the street would already be crawling with uniforms, or at least a cruiser would have rolled slowly by. Lou Dawg was certain. Their people were monitoring his calls, his texts. If Beck had reached for a lifeline, it would have had to be a phone they couldn't see. A burner. But looking at the man's restless pacing, Lou Dawg doubted he had that kind of foresight.

He took a drag, exhaled smoke toward the cracked window. The cigarette burned low, leaving a bitter taste on his tongue. He flicked the ash into an empty coffee cup and studied Caldwell again. The lawyer was unraveling and Lou Dawg knew it. Good men always did when you squeezed them hard enough. They carried reputations, clients, consciences, all leverage in the right hands. They were unaccustomed to the seedy underbelly where he lived and breathed.

Chico stirred, stretched, and gave a low whine. Lou Dawg

scratched the dog's ears absently, his eyes never leaving the casita. "Easy," he muttered. "He's not going anywhere."

Caldwell sat on the couch and thought of the *blue glass*. Where was Holly and why was she trying to give him information about blue glass? He reached in his pocket and removed her phone. Hackers couldn't watch everything, could they? He had to believe there was a crack in their net, someplace he could slip through without being noticed. He wouldn't use the phone. Not yet.

His thumb hovered over the screen before he swiped it open. The battery was low, but alive. He went to the photos, scrolling through the gallery she'd left behind. There were pictures of their past trips to the Southwest, notes for her articles, snapshots she always took of little details. Old doors, street musicians, adobe walls painted in fading murals. Then he stopped.

Basketry. Several shots of coiled baskets, tightly woven, the strands precise. But what caught his breath were the glints embedded in the reeds, shards of cobalt and turquoise, glass pieces flashing like trapped lights. Blue glass. Holly had taken close-ups, framing the pieces so that the fragments glittered like stars caught in a net. He remembered that she had included them in her article about that particular trip to Santa Fe two years before.

Caldwell leaned closer, tapping one photo to expand it. The weaver's hands were visible, brown and strong, caught mid-motion as she pressed a strip of reed tight against the rim. The caption Holly had typed beneath it read: Santo Domingo artisan, Luz G.

His pulse quickened. He backed out of the photos and into

her internet browser. It felt like trespassing, but the urgency left no room for hesitation. He found it. An article popped up about a local artist. Luz Gutierrez, basket weaver, Kewa Santo Domingo Pueblo Tribe. The line of text named her reservation, the Cochiti Reservation, an hour southwest of Santa Fe.

Caldwell sat back, the phone trembling in his hand. Blue glass wasn't random. Holly hadn't been talking about a gallery window or a sculpture in the Plaza, she'd been telling him about Luz, about the baskets, about where she might be.

He set the phone down carefully on the coffee table, as if afraid to spook the information he'd just uncovered. His breath came shallow, quick. He had a name. He had a place. For the first time, he had a trail.

CHAPTER SEVEN

aldwell didn't risk using the map app on Holly's phone. He went through a large basket of tourist information provided by the hosts of the Airbnb and found what he was looking for. A map of the area showing the Turquoise Trail and how it snaked down toward Albuquerque. He located the Cochiti Reservation, about an hour's drive away, and tore the map out of the guide. He grabbed his coat and his keys and ran toward the SUV.

He took several sharp turns around Santa Fe watching his rearview mirror and could not tell if he was being followed. *I'll have to risk it.*

He left the populated area and wound his way through hills and canyons until he found the appropriate highway as it grew darker. The map was adorned with pictures of various tourist places along the way, but those were all closed at night.

His heart ached for Holly. How could he ever let so many petty things come between them? What importance were they now? He remembered how they'd met in Houston. He could see her smiling face in his memory.

Caldwell had gone reluctantly. His partners insisted their presence at fundraisers was good business. Clients liked to see attorneys as cultured patrons of the arts, not just courtroom gladiators.

The downtown Houston gallery had been transformed into something warmer than its steel-and-glass bones usually allowed. Strings of light floated from the rafters, and the air hummed with conversation. Sculptures and photographs lined the walls, pieces Holly had identified during her travels: woven baskets from New Mexico, a series of desert landscapes from West Texas, a splash of color from a muralist in Oaxaca. The fundraiser carried the law firm's name, as sponsor, in bold letters on the program, but the artistry was hers.

He'd donned his best gray suit, arrived late, and shaken a few hands, but after fifteen minutes he found himself drifting toward a quiet corner where a terra cotta bowl caught the light and held it.

"Beautiful, isn't it?" a voice said beside him.

He turned. She stood there with a glass of sparkling wine in her hand, her blonde hair pinned up loosely, eyes lit with something brighter than the art itself.

"Yeah," Caldwell said, nodding toward the piece. "It's... different. Hard to stop looking at."

"That's the idea." She smiled, a quick knowing curve of her lips. "The artist embeds gold into the clay, so it fractures when fired. What you're looking at is imperfection that turned out better than the original plan."

Caldwell chuckled. "I could use more of that in my line of work."

"And what line of work is that?"

"Law," he admitted. "Oil and gas litigation. Not exactly as interesting as fractured clay pots."

Her brows lifted. "So, you're one of the sponsors."

"Guilty." He hesitated, then offered his hand. "Caldwell Beck."

She shook it, her grip firm, her eyes steady. "Holly Rowe. Curator of this little gathering."

"Curator?" He glanced around at the displays. "Then you're responsible for making me look cultured tonight."

Her laugh was soft but genuine. "If you can talk about clay and gold for thirty seconds, you'll pass. I'm also a travel writer, and these are pieces by artists I've written about over the years."

He grinned. "Thanks for the lifeline." He let the moment breathe, then added, "I have to say, the way you described it, it sounded more like a philosophy than an art technique."

"Maybe it is," she said, tilting her head. "Sometimes what breaks is more beautiful than what you planned."

Caldwell had studied her, the spark in her words, the warmth in her tone. He realized the fundraiser wasn't just a box to check for his firm. It was the start of something he hadn't seen coming.

"Would you," he asked, carefully, "consider telling me more about imperfect art over dinner sometime? I promise not to act too much like a lawyer."

She smiled again, this time softer, a smile that felt like it had been saved just for him. "I think I'd like that, Counselor."

Later, on one of their many dates, Caldwell learned that Holly Rowe had never been the kind of writer who wanted to cover hard news or politics.

From the beginning, she chased color, texture, and the way light hit unexpected corners of the world. Her love of unusual art had started back in her undergraduate days at the Savannah School of Design, where she majored in visual culture. She'd fallen in love with the small galleries tucked into alleyways, the artisans who carved meaning into wood, glass, or clay, and the way their work reflected the places they came from.

Her professors encouraged her to keep journals on field trips, and those notes often grew into essays. She was less interested in critique than in the story behind the work: the potter whose grandmother had taught him to shape clay by a river, the weaver who wove family history into patterns. Holly's writing wasn't just about art, it was about people. About the thread that tied identity to creation.

After graduation, she'd taken a handful of internships at glossy travel magazines. She learned quickly that the work wasn't glamorous: long hours fact-checking, transcribing other people's interviews, hustling to pitch stories that would never get approved. But freelancing gave her freedom. She could follow her instincts, take assignments on unique galleries in New Mexico one month and profile an outsider artist in Marfa, Texas, the next.

Houston wasn't the obvious place for a freelance travel and art writer to land, but life had a way of bending practical. She'd followed a boyfriend there initially, an engineer who promised stability. The relationship fizzled, but Houston stuck. It had a thriving art scene. It was cheaper than New York, more connected than Santa Fe, and busy enough to keep her assignments flowing. From there, she could travel, short hops to Austin, quick flights to Denver, and still have a base with enough Wi-Fi and coffee shops to support a freelancer's life.

Over time, she built a reputation for finding stories others overlooked. Editors knew that if Holly pitched something, it would come back layered, part travelogue, part human portrait, always with a detail that lingered. A string of bylines followed in online magazines and print quarterlies. She wasn't famous, but she had her niche and she lived in it happily.

What anchored her, though, wasn't just the writing, it was the hunt for beauty in unexpected places. Whether it was a cracked piece of cobalt glass embedded in a silver bracelet or the faded paint on a road sign along Route 66, Holly Rowe had an eye for the small things that told the biggest stories.

As time went by, Caldwell learned that Holly had the kind of presence that turned heads without trying. Her hair was a natural blonde, long and silky, catching the light in soft waves that framed her face. She carried herself with an easy poise that spoke of confidence, all clean lines and quiet grace.

Her blue-gray eyes were striking and alert, intelligent, always measuring the room. Beneath their brightness was the edge of a journalist, someone who had seen enough of the world to know beauty could be a mask as much as a gift.

She dressed simply—dark jeans, tailored jackets, soft sweaters—clothes that didn't beg for attention yet managed to accentuate her shape. But what made her unforgettable wasn't just her looks. It was the energy, warmth when she smiled, fire when she was cornered, and a sharpness of wit that made it clear she was no ornament on Caldwell's arm. She was his equal, his balance, the one who grounded him.

It was impossible for Caldwell to believe he'd never see her again. His heart was full of regret and self-blame but mostly love. He realized, for the first time, he loved her more than his own life.

Lou Dawg's Ford rattled as he steered it along the highway, a few car lengths behind Caldwell's SUV. He kept his headlights low, far enough back to look like any other late-night traveler but close enough to keep Caldwell's taillights pinned in his vision.

"Where the hell is he going?" Lou Dawg asked Chico snoring on the passenger seat, oblivious to the cold rolling in from the cracked window.

They left the city glow behind, the lights of Santa Fe shrinking in the rearview. The land stretched dark and flat, only broken by mesas and the occasional flicker of a passing vehicle. Lou Dawg tapped ash into a coffee cup and muttered under his breath.

They wove through the countryside until Caldwell turned onto the main road to the reservation.

"Oh, hell no. He didn't figure out where she is. How?"

When Beck slowed to make the turn into the Cochiti Reservation, Lou Dawg cursed softly and picked up his phone. He speed dialed Santa's number with one hand, the wheel steady under the other. The line clicked alive, Santa's rasp sharp even through the static.

"It's me. He's on the move," Lou Dawg said. "Headed south. And get this, he just turned off for the reservation. Caldwell Beck found the Cochiti."

There was a pause, the sound of a breath dragging slow. "You're certain?"

"Following him right now," Lou Dawg said. "He's driving through the reservation."

"You told me you were discreet," Santa growled.

Lou Dawg saw Caldwell slow and cut his lights.

"He must've put the clues together about my mother and the blue glass. I can't think of anything else. But he can't seem to find my trailer. He's stopping now and getting out. I'll park in the hills and go in on foot."

Another pause, longer this time. Then Santa's voice dropped, a quiet slice of steel.

"If he finds her, grab him, too. We'll force him to do the legal work, then put them both down. It's not ideal. I'd like to keep him on the case, but we can't risk him leading the cops to us if we let him go. I'm on my way now. It will take me about an hour."

Lou Dawg tightened his grip on the wheel, then eased behind an outcropping of rock.

"Copy that." He hung up.

"Let's go, Chico." He took an industrial-size flashlight from the glove box and got out. The chihuahua barked once then quieted as if he knew the routine. He trotted out into the desert to relieve himself, then followed along behind his master.

Lou Dawg smiled thinly in the dark. What Caldwell didn't know was that answers had a way of turning into traps.

The desert road stretched dark and empty, the headlights of Caldwell's SUV slowly cutting a narrow path through sagebrush and scrub. The reservation vast and unfamiliar, each curve more like guesswork than progress. He scanned the horizon for lights but saw nothing. The outcroppings blocked what few buildings were farther into the land. Finally, several miles in, he pulled over onto the shoulder, gravel crunching under the tires.

Caldwell stepped out into the cold night. The silence pressed against him, broken only by the running engine. Overhead, stars spilled across the black sky, brighter than anything he'd seen in Houston. He fumbled Holly's phone from his pocket, lifted it high, searching for a signal. A single bar flickered, then died.

"Come on," he muttered, swiping to refresh the map. Then, he tried for internet access to search for a map of the reservation. Something, anything that would point to Holly. No luck. The blue dot blinked, uncertain, then vanished again. He dropped the phone into his pocket and looked out across the desert. Scanning. Searching.

He was so focused on trying to find anything with lights on, he didn't hear the crunch of boots behind him.

A shadow moved quickly, and then—

CRACK.

Pain exploded across the back of Caldwell's skull. He staggered forward. The night spun. He tried to turn, to raise a hand in defense, but another blow to his shoulder landed hard and his knees buckled.

The last thing he saw before darkness swallowed him was the faint glow of Holly's face in his memory.

Lou Dawg stood over him, an unlit cigarette dangling from his lips, the flashlight still warm in his hand. Lou Dawg bent, grabbed Caldwell under the arms, and hauled his limp body toward the SUV.

"Should've stayed in town, Counselor," he muttered.

He popped the hatch of the SUV, heaved Caldwell inside, and slammed it shut with a dull thud. Dust lifted from the road as Lou Dawg climbed behind the wheel, lit the cigarette, and started the engine, leaving his truck hidden by the entrance.

He pulled the SUV back onto the dirt road, driving deeper into the reservation. With each mile, the stars gave way to darkness, until the headlights picked out the lonely outline of Lou Dawg's trailer, waiting in the distance like a mouth at the end of the road.

CHAPTER EIGHT

The SUV bounced over the rutted dirt road, its shocks groaning with every dip. In the hatch, Caldwell stirred, pain hammering at the base of his skull. His eyelids fluttered against the dark, the tang of blood and carpet fibers thick in his nose. He raised a hand, surprised to find his wrists weren't bound.

Maybe he thinks I'm dead.

He pushed up on one elbow, head swimming. The road was rough, the bumps pressing him hard against the sides of the SUV. Every jolt rattled through his bruises. He felt around the hatch for a weapon but found nothing useful. He rolled against the back of the seats and lifted the spare tire cover enough to get his hand underneath. He felt the jack secured next to the spare but couldn't find the tire iron.

This will have to do.

His fingers curled around it, desperate, the weight anchoring his fogged mind and giving him a surge of focus.

From the front of the SUV came a strange contrast to the violence of the ride. The crackle of the local radio station cut through the groan of the engine. Burl Ives' voice spilled out in warm, syrupy tones: *Have a holly, jolly Christmas...* The cheerful croon wove through the dark like a taunt.

Caldwell's jaw clenched. Christmas music in the middle of a desert kidnapping. Madness.

He waited for the next heavy jolt, braced himself, then shoved the back seat lever down and crawled forward into the cabin. Lou Dawg's broad head bobbed just feet away, framed by the green glow of the dash lights.

Caldwell rose from the shadows like a ghost and swung. The heavy jack whistled, missed clean, and smashed into the seat back, glancing off Lou Dawg's shoulder.

"What the hell?" Lou Dawg snarled, jerking the wheel. The SUV fishtailed, dirt spraying in arcs.

Caldwell lunged again, wrapping one arm around Lou Dawg's thick neck, the jack pressed under his chin. The bigger man roared, muscles knotting under Caldwell's grip, one hand fighting the wheel, the other clamping on to Caldwell's wrist in a crushing vise.

"Son of a—" Lou Dawg spat, teeth bared. He drove his elbow backward, catching Caldwell square in the jaw. The blow knocked him flat. The SUV veered, headlights carving wild arcs through the dark hills, briefly illuminating sagebrush and the jagged silhouettes of boulders.

Before Lou Dawg could pull over, Caldwell climbed back up, jack in hand, and hit him in the head. For a heartbeat he thought he had him. The man's head snapped sideways, his grip on the wheel faltering. The SUV lurched off-road, tires grinding rock and dirt.

But Lou Dawg was stronger. He twisted the wheel with brute force, slamming Caldwell sideways into the back door. He braked hard.

Caldwell knew he couldn't win. Not head-on. Not against

this monster. He did the only thing left. He yanked the door handle and rolled as the SUV came to a stop.

Caldwell hit the dirt hard, the impact rattling his teeth. He tumbled down a slope, scraping rocks and scrub tearing at his jacket and skin, before he came to rest in a cloud of choking dust mixed with patches of unmelted snow.

Above him, Lou Dawg continued to curse as the radio blared on, Christmas bells jangling against the night. The driver's door flew open as Lou Dawg grabbed the still bloody flashlight.

"Beck!" the voice bellowed, deep and furious, echoing across the desert.

Caldwell scrambled into the shadows, lungs burning, heart pounding. He ducked into a narrow cut between two boulders and pressed himself flat, grit biting into his palms.

A beam of light sliced across the hillside. Once, twice, searching. Lou Dawg's boots crunched on stone. The flashlight beam stabbed closer. Caldwell inched deeper into a thorny juniper, the branches raking his arms. He closed his eyes, praying Lou Dawg's fury wouldn't harden into patience.

Minutes dragged like hours. Lou Dawg cursed again, loud and sharp, the sound cutting through the stillness. Then the beam swept away. Footsteps stomped back to the SUV.

The door slammed. The engine roared. Burl Ives picked up where he left off, syrupy and wrong: *It's the best time of the year...*

Headlights swung forward, climbing the road toward a faint glow of a trailer in the distance.

Caldwell didn't move until the sound dwindled and silence reclaimed the hills. He sagged back against the cold earth, trembling, the stars above sharp and endless, then tried to stand.

Alive. Loose in the desert. With nothing but dust, stars, and his own battered will for company.

Lou Dawg hadn't finished with him. But for now, Caldwell had slipped the noose.

The desert lay silent after the SUV's engine cut off. Caldwell crouched low behind a rise, listening to the tick of the motor cooling in the night air. It was his SUV, still in Lou Dawg's hands. The Ford truck was miles back, abandoned at the reservation entrance where Lou Dawg had switched to Caldwell's vehicle.

Only the SUV sat outside the trailer, parked crooked on bare dirt, headlights dimming to orange before they clicked off. With what little light there was, Caldwell could not see another road or trail. It appeared there was only one way out, back the way they'd come.

The trailer itself leaned tiredly on its cinder block foundation, aluminum siding dented and streaked with rust. One back window glowed faintly, curtains half drawn. A strand of dusty holiday lights sagged across the front porch, half the bulbs dead, the rest casting a weak red and green shimmer across the metal. The desert wind teased them, making them rattle like bones.

Caldwell moved along the siding to the rear, every muscle aching, until he reached the glowing window. He eased up and looked inside.

Holly.

She lay on a narrow bed in the back room, wrists bound in front of her, ankles tied together, a strip of duct tape pressed across her mouth. Her blonde hair clung to her cheeks, streaked with sweat and tears.

The small bedroom held little else but the bed, a crooked dresser, and the sagging curtain on the only window. The walls bore water stains like bruises. The chihuahua mix jumped up on the bed beside her.

Lou Dawg stood in the doorway, his shadow long across the floor. His voice was low, cruel, but clear enough for Caldwell to catch every word.

"Your boyfriend's dead. Now you're screwed."

Holly's body tensed. Her eyes squeezed shut, tears welling fresh. She hid her pain by turning away from Lou Dawg.

Then, she saw him.

Caldwell, face streaked with blood and dust, staring back through the glass. Alive.

Her muffled sobs shifted, part cry, part gasp, as her eyes widened. Hope and terror collided in them.

Lou Dawg didn't notice. He bent, flicked open a pocketknife, and sawed through the rope around her ankles. The coarse fiber snapped. He grabbed her by the arm, hauling her up off the mattress.

"Time to move."

The bedsprings creaked as she staggered to her feet. He shoved her forward, steering her out of the bedroom and into the narrow hall. The linoleum cracked and popped under their boots, hollow sounds echoing in the thin-walled trailer.

From the window, Caldwell pressed a bloody palm against the glass. He couldn't stop Lou Dawg yet. Couldn't risk it. But Holly had seen him and that spark in her eyes told him what mattered most.

She knew. He had come for her.

CHAPTER NINE

The trailer door screeched open on its rusted hinges. Lou Dawg shoved Holly out first into the biting cold, her wrists still bound, duct tape silver across her mouth. She stumbled down the warped wooden steps, catching herself before she fell. The cold night air hit her face, and she shivered hard. He grabbed her arm roughly and marched her to the SUV.

Caldwell crouched behind a mesquite bush fifteen yards off, every muscle clenched. The SUV sat in the dirt just ahead of him. The weak glow of the Christmas bulbs sagged above the trailer, flickering red and green over the scene like some sick holiday diorama.

Lou Dawg yanked the SUV's hatch open and shoved Holly inside. She landed on the cover, her shoulder striking the doorframe with a muffled cry. He pulled a length of rope from his waistband and re-tied her ankles. He slammed the hatch shut, the echo sharp against the empty desert.

Caldwell's pulse hammered. So close. If he rushed it now,

Lou Dawg would tear him apart. He slid lower in the brush, dust sticking to the sweat on his face. Watching and waiting.

Lou Dawg leaned against the SUV, pulled out his phone, and speed dialed a number with thick fingers. The screen glowed pale across his scarred knuckles.

"Santa," Lou Dawg said, breath loud in the quiet. "It's done. Caldwell's out there somewhere. Dead, probably. I got the girl. 'Bout to get rid of her."

The reply came faint but sharp, Santa's voice carrying even through the tinny speaker.

"Are you out of your mind? That wasn't the plan."

Lou Dawg straightened, jaw tight. "The plan went to hell. He came at me from behind. Nearly brained me. I had no choice but to fight back."

"You told me you had it handled," Santa snapped. "Now you've got a mess. GulfTex is breathing down my neck, and you think dumping her fixes it?"

Lou Dawg's face twisted. "She's dead weight. The lawyer's gone. No point keeping her. Maybe we can grab someone else from his office."

"No," Santa barked, his voice sharp as glass. "You wait there. Don't move her. I'm on my way."

Lou Dawg growled low, pacing in the dirt. "Whole thing's gone sideways."

"Shut up and sit tight," Santa said. "Do not make this worse. It won't take me much longer. I'm halfway there."

The call ended. Lou Dawg spat into the dust and kicked the SUV's tire. He leaned against the hood, staring off into the black hills, pouting.

From the brush, Caldwell exhaled silently. He'd just been handed one thing he needed most: time. But time wouldn't last.

He circled wide, crouching low, moving in a half-moon arc

toward the rear of the SUV. The desert gave him little cover, just scrub and shadow. Each step was a gamble. The crunch of gravel under his boots felt like thunder.

Inside the vehicle, Holly shifted. Through the glass, her eyes darted, frantic, searching. Caldwell froze, then raised his head slowly. Her gaze locked on his. Her eyes widened.

She knew he was there.

Caldwell ducked again and pressed lower to the dirt, every nerve alive. He was close enough to hear Lou Dawg's boots scraping the gravel, close enough to smell the sour tang of sweat and cigarettes that drifted from the bigger man's clothes.

Too close to make a mistake.

Caldwell sank lower into the shadows, knees pressed in the dirt. Lou Dawg finished his cigarette, ground it into the gravel with his boot, walked over, and yanked open the trailer door.

"Stay put, girl," he barked toward the SUV, his voice rough with irritation.

The door slammed behind him, the trailer groaning on its blocks as he disappeared inside.

Caldwell crept forward, slipping along the aluminum siding until he reached the trailer's end. He crouched in the shadows where the porch light didn't shine, every nerve taut, listening.

The trailer's thin walls carried every sound. Lou Dawg's heavy steps thudded inside, drawers opening and slamming shut. A few minutes later, the door banged open again. Lou Dawg stomped down the steps, a battered suitcase in one hand. He went to the SUV and opened the back door on the driver's side.

Caldwell exhaled. This was it.

As Lou Dawg threw the bag carelessly into the back seat, Caldwell darted around the far end of the trailer and slipped through the door Lou Dawg had left open. The air inside hit him at once. Stale smoke, spilled beer, fried grease baked into the walls. He grabbed a kitchen knife off the counter and continued to look around for a better weapon.

The living room was cramped: a stained couch sagging in the middle, a scarred coffee table littered with beer cans and cigarette butts. On the wall above the couch hung a mounted rack of deer horns. Antlers were nailed to cheap paneling. Beneath them, a rifle rested on a wooden gun rack.

Caldwell's chest tightened.

As he listened for Lou Dawg's return, he crossed the room in three strides, hands trembling as he pocketed the knife and lifted the hunting rifle free. He eased down the hall backward, watching the open door. He checked the chamber with fingers that remembered the motion by heart. A round slid smoothly into place. Loaded.

For the first time since this nightmare began, he felt a spark of control.

"Thanks, Dad," he whispered, voice dry. His father's voice came back to him from a childhood dawn in a deer blind: *Always know your weapon. Always respect it. And never aim unless you're ready to pull the trigger.*

He brought the rifle to his shoulder, testing the weight. Heavy, solid, reliable.

Outside, the sound of Lou Dawg's boots crunched gravel again.

Caldwell backed farther into the shadows of the hallway, rifle tight against his chest, breath locked in his lungs.

When Caldwell heard Lou Dawg take the first step onto the porch, he made his move. The trailer porch groaned as Caldwell stepped out, rifle braced against his shoulder, the barrel trained squarely on Lou Dawg.

"Step away from the porch," Caldwell said, his voice sharp, iron edged.

Lou Dawg backed up, then froze halfway between the porch and the SUV, his shoulders hunching. Then slowly, a grin stretched across his battered face. "Well, look who crawled outta the grave. Thought I left you feedin' coyotes."

"Guess you thought wrong," Caldwell said. "Hands where I can see them."

Lou Dawg spread his arms wide, mockery in every motion. "You don't have the stones to pull that trigger, Beck. You're a courthouse cowboy, not a killer."

Caldwell took a step down off the porch, rifle steady. "You want to test that theory?"

Lou Dawg's smile thinned, his eyes darkening. "You got lucky finding that gun. But me? I'll take it from you, shove the barrel down your throat, and paint the dirt with your brains."

"Shut up," Caldwell snapped, the rifle never wavering. "Back up. Toward the SUV. Now."

The bigger man snorted but obeyed, shuffling backward, boots grinding gravel. He lifted his hands higher, though his eyes glittered with calculation.

"Pop always said never trust a gun in soft hands," Lou Dawg taunted. "You'll fumble it, and I'll break you in half."

"Keep talking," Caldwell said, his jaw clenched. "I've been hunting since I was twelve. All you're doing is proving what you are, a hired thug too dumb to know when he's beat."

They reached the SUV, both men on high alert. Holly's wide eyes shone through the rear glass, her forehead pressed against it, duct tape still gagging her mouth.

"Open it," Caldwell ordered and gestured with the gun toward the hatch.

Lou Dawg hesitated. "You sure you want her out? Makes her a target. Easier if I just…"

The rifle muzzle nudged forward. "Do it. Now."

For a long moment, the desert held its breath. Then Lou Dawg cursed and yanked the hatch release. The SUV's back lifted with a creak.

"Now, back up." Caldwell gestured again with the rifle.

Lou Dawg took a step away from the hatch.

Caldwell's gaze flicked to Holly. "Come on, Holly. You're safe now."

Lou Dawg sneered. "Ain't safe till I say she's safe."

"On your knees," Caldwell barked.

For once, Lou Dawg had no smart remark as he obeyed.

Caldwell shifted the rifle with one hand, the other reaching into the hatch. His fingers tore at the duct tape, peeling it free from Holly's mouth. She gasped, her first words breaking out as a sob: "Caldwell—"

He kept the rifle on Lou Dawg and withdrew the kitchen knife from his pocket. She sliced the rope across the blade at her wrists, the fibers falling away. She took the knife from his hand and cut the rope at her ankles. When she was released, she threw her arms around Caldwell's neck, shaking, clinging like she'd never let go.

"You're alive," she whispered, her voice ragged. "How?"

He kept one eye on Lou Dawg. "It was the blue glass," he said, pressing the side of his head against hers, the rifle still tight in his hands. His body shook, not from fear now but fury and relief tangled together.

Before them, Lou Dawg chuckled low, even on his knees. "Ain't over, Beck. Santa's comin'. And when he gets here, you're both dead."

Caldwell leveled the rifle squarely at Lou Dawg's head as Holly hung on to his arm. "Then I guess I'll just have to make sure you don't live long enough to see him. Now, get in the trailer."

CHAPTER TEN

aldwell shoved Lou Dawg through the trailer door hard enough that the cheap hinges groaned. The big man hit the sagging linoleum with a grunt and folded forward, hands skittering on the floor. Caldwell's rifle never left his side; the barrel tracked every twitch.

"Sit," Caldwell said, voice flat. Lou Dawg got up, and Caldwell shoved him into a rickety chair by the coffee table. Holly, eyes furious and wet, moved without being told. She found a length of cord from the roll Lou Dawg had used to tie her up.

"Let's see how you like it." She was careful to stay out of his grasp as she bound his torso to the back of the chair. Her fingers working with a sureness that steadied Caldwell more than the rifle ever could.

She went behind him, pulled his hands behind the chair, looped the cord twice around his wrists, cinched it tight. Then she bound his ankles, threaded the cord through a rung and pulled it in. She worked fast, efficiently, and when she finished, she stepped back, breathing hard.

"Don't," Lou Dawg started, but Holly's foot came up and planted in his groin. He slumped forward. She smiled with revenge.

Caldwell lowered the rifle from his shoulder but kept his hand on it. "Now, let's talk."

Lou Dawg tried to sit back and make a joke of it. "You think you're some kind of hero?" But the laugh died in his throat when Caldwell's boot kicked his knee and the reality of who had the gun settled again. Sweat stood on his forehead. The man who'd swaggered in the trailer was shrinking under the thin bulb's light.

For a long second only Holly's breathing and the trailer's faint creak answered. Then Caldwell stepped close, close enough that Lou Dawg could see the cuts on his face and smell the desert and blood and everything that had gone into getting here.

"Who is Santa?" Caldwell demanded.

"Wouldn't you like to know," Lou Dawg grunted.

Caldwell propped the gun against the wall, curled his hand into a fist, and let it fly. One hard, unpracticed strike across Lou Dawg's jaw that wasn't meant to maim but to make the man listen.

"Who is Santa?" Caldwell repeated. His voice was gravel and winter; it cut. "Tell me who he works for. Tell me how GulfTex is involved."

Lou Dawg's head lolled to the side where Holly had tangled his braided hair with the cord; his mouth opened, a red smear across his lips. He spat blood and tried to smile, a wet, animal grin.

"You wanna know? You wanna know and cry about it after?" he rasped. "You been in the dirt long enough, lawyer. Ain't no savin' you. You already broke all your vows."

"Talk," Caldwell said. "Now."

The world narrowed to the man in the chair and the woman he'd kidnapped. Lou Dawg's eyes flicked to Holly. Something like shame or regret crossed his face for a heartbeat and then he shrugged as if weightless.

"What do I get if I tell you?"

"You get to live, and you might get some help from the local police."

"Tribal Police only on the res. No local police here."

"You know the Feds have authority here, too. Tribal Police might be glad to rid themselves of you anyway. Now talk."

Lou Dawg's wrists burned where the rope dug in. The nylon was slick with sweat, his own blood starting to bead where he'd twisted too hard. He glared at Caldwell across the dim trailer, the little lamp by the sink throwing yellow light on the lawyer's face. Caldwell's jacket was torn at the shoulder, his jaw set tight as he leveled the rifle.

"You're gonna tell me," Caldwell said. "Now."

Lou Dawg swallowed hard, working his tongue over dry lips. His mind spun like a busted fan.

He could roll on Santa, but Santa wasn't the type to forgive a snitch. GulfTex would know before dawn. Those boys had tentacles everywhere. If he gave up Santa, he'd be a dead man before sunrise. If he didn't cooperate, the Feds would sniff around the res and they'd pin half the operation on him if they could.

Then there were the tribal cops—two of them had been itching to haul him in since he was a kid. They'd love to parade him through the station, slap a "cooperating witness" tag on him, and dump him into Federal custody. He'd never make it through a week in holding.

Caldwell trained the rifle on Lou Dawg.

Lou Dawg looked up at Caldwell. The man was a mess, but his eyes were cold—Texas courtroom cold. Lou Dawg had seen that kind of calm before, right before things got bloody.

He weighed his choices. Run his mouth and die slowly. Keep it shut and maybe die quicker.

"Clock's ticking, Lou," Caldwell said, voice low but steady.

Lou Dawg smirked through the pain. "You think I'm scared of you, lawyer boy? You don't know what you're pokin' at. If Santa hears I even breathed his name—well, let's just say I'd wish you'd left me out there in the dirt."

Caldwell didn't flinch. He took a slow step closer. "We can make that happen right here." He looked like he could kill someone.

Lou Dawg stared back, every possible exit slamming shut in his head. For the first time, he realized the only way out of this trailer might be feet first. Maybe if he talked, he'd get another chance to break free and run. He had enough money to make it for a while. Maybe Santa would be too late or think he was dead in the desert. Maybe.

"All right," he said hoarsely. "Santa ain't no Santa. That's what they call him 'cause he brings gifts, if you know what I mean. Real name's George Saint. Runs the dirty stuff for Gulf-Tex. Been doin' it for years. You do a favor for the company, he makes sure you eat good afterwards. You cross 'em, he makes you disappear slow."

Holly's hand rose, a small, involuntary motion. Caldwell's chest tightened.

"How long have you been working with Santa?"

"Not long, just a few jobs over the last year or two. Nothing this big. I ain't going down for him, that's for sure."

Caldwell asked. "How long has Santa been working for GulfTex?"

Lou Dawg swallowed. "Years. He's like their fixer. Not on

the books, cash only. Boots on the ground, you know? You need someone buried, someone intimidated, someone scared off, Santa handles it. He pulls strings with guys he trusts. He has a whole network of contractors. I'm just one of them. Most of the time, he doesn't do his own wet work, but if he has to, he gets his hands dirty. GulfTex likes quiet. They pay for quiet."

Caldwell's fists tightened until his knuckles blanched around the rifle trained on Lou Dawg. He thought of depositions, of court files, of witnesses whose lives could be ruined by a well-placed threat. He thought of his client, how much Johnson had at risk. He considered the information Lou Dawg had that could sink a company like GulfTex. The arithmetic of why Lou Dawg was so afraid came clear.

"Why'd you take her instead of me? I'm the one who can get into the court records."

Lou Dawg's grin was wobbly, as if the joke tasted wrong. "Yeah. Boss said make him listen. Make him fold. We were supposed to make you do something. Make you look like a screwup. GulfTex pays Santa, they get their motion, Johnson's case goes to trial. That's business."

Holly's jaw tightened. Her hands flew to her mouth as if she could still feel the tape there. Caldwell's eyes snapped to her and back to Lou Dawg.

"And your instructions?" Caldwell pressed. "What did he tell you to do if I refused?"

Lou Dawg's laugh had a cracked edge. "If you refused, boss said keep her. Send pictures. Put pressure. If he still stonewalls, get rid of her. He don't want no loose ends. Company don't want heat. Sometimes they can make disappearances look like accidents, you catch my drift. You'd never know who me or Santa was and couldn't prove who we worked for."

A cold, slow fury spread through Caldwell like oil. He thought about what "pressure" had already meant in the court and how close he'd come to being unmade. Holly's life had been currency in the exchange.

"He lives most of the time in Lubbock, near the oil patch. It's a few hours' drive over here. He's on his way now," Lou Dawg lied.

"Who in GulfTex called him in on this? Who's the contact?"

Lou Dawg's face crumpled. "I only know Santa. Said they were sweating the Johnson suit. Said make sure Beck..." He coughed. "Make sure Beck folds."

"You're lying," Caldwell said flatly.

Lou Dawg's eyes flicked like a trapped animal's. "You think I wanna be the one sayin' it? You think it matters? I'm just a man with a job. I get paid to follow orders. I don't ask why. I don't do the numbers. I do the heavy work. Santa runs the show on the ground. GulfTex signs the checks."

Caldwell propped the rifle against the wall and looked at Holly. She was clear eyed. Caldwell's fist found Lou Dawg's chest. Two hard hits, meant to jar more than to cripple. The man slumped deeper against the chair. "You picked the wrong guy's woman," Caldwell said. "You picked the wrong place to play games. You don't get to call this work."

Lou Dawg spat a little blood and, in a voice suddenly small, said, "Santa's on his way. He'll clean this up. You don't got time to dig into me. Move now, Beck, or you're both dead. Probably me, too."

The words were a warning and a threat. Caldwell let them hang. Caldwell felt the clock ticking. Santa was on his way. GulfTex's puppeteers still didn't have names, but the board of directors wasn't hard to find. There were places to go and people to warn and a web of leverage that went deeper than he'd probably guessed. He needed more information, but he was running out of time.

He let his hand find Lou Dawg's shoulder wound and squeezed until the man flinched. "Names. I want names."

Lou Dawg's eyes slid left and right like someone looking for an exit.

"I'm telling you. I don't know anyone but Santa. They wouldn't trust me with important info. I'm just the muscle."

When Lou Dawg finished, his voice a collapsing thing, Caldwell kept his hand steady. He looked past the man to Holly, her chin raised, eyes fierce, hands in her lap. She'd tied the man up. She'd helped make him small. Caldwell wanted to make sure she had her say.

"You believe him?" Caldwell asked Holly.

"Yeah, he's too stupid to be anything more than the hired help."

Caldwell grabbed the rifle and sat, the gun balanced on his knee like a promise. The desert night pressed in around the trailer wind whispered. He took a deep breath.

Outside, somewhere on the black ribbon of road, an engine hummed. The tense little kingdom Caldwell had carved out inside the trailer held for now, but he knew the fragile safety could break with the next set of headlights.

He breathed in, nodded to Holly, and got to his feet.

"Get the SUV keys," he said, voice low. "We need to bring in the authorities, and we don't know when Santa left Lubbock or when he might be here."

It was the one thing Lou Dawg had lied about. Santa was closer than they knew.

The trailer hummed with a silence that felt brittle as glass. Holly moved to the chair where Lou Dawg sagged and fished his phone from his pocket. The screen lit, three bars, LTE, a small miracle in the middle of nowhere.

Caldwell watched the yard through the window, every part of him keyed to the dark. The single ribbon of gravel that cut through this end of the reservation was the only way in or out, straight and exposed. If anyone came, this was the lane they'd use. No back routes, no clever service roads, no neat escapes.

"I've got the path mapped," Holly said, reading the map on the screen and then looking back at him. Her voice was steady but thin. "We go out the only way. We call the police when we're near the exit of the reservation."

Caldwell nodded. The choice narrowed the options and sharpened the danger. If Santa was coming in, he'd see the SUV. But sitting here under the trailer's dim bulb felt like waiting for a verdict you couldn't negotiate.

"All right," he said. "We take the SUV. Take his phone and his truck keys. We leave him here, tied. Santa can deal with him. We get off the res road as fast as we can and call people who won't sell us out."

Holly went back to the bedroom, went into the closet, and took one of Lou Dawg's jackets. It was more like a cape than a coat, but she rolled up the sleeves and made it work.

She went back to the living room, jammed the phone and keys into a jacket pocket, and took pleasure in pasting a strip of duct tape across Lou Dawg's mouth. For a second she looked at him, small and furious and human, and then she turned away.

Holly drove so Caldwell could hang on to the rifle. She eased the SUV out of the dirt yard. The trailer's sagging Christmas bulbs winked once in the rearview and then went dark behind them. Dust rose in a low cloud that swallowed the porch and the bound man within seconds.

As they pulled out on to the gravel road, the night seemed to rearrange itself around them. It felt open, exposed, unforgiving. They didn't pass a single vehicle as the gravel turned to asphalt. As they continued toward the exit, they didn't see anyone.

Holly kept her hands tight on the wheel. Caldwell's throat worked. They had to make the stretch between the trailer and reservation exit without being noticed. The SUV's headlights outlined the mesas, painted the world in hard white.

When they'd put a mile between themselves and the trailer, Holly dug the phone out from the pocket. The bars were holding. She found, then thumbed a number and handed it to Caldwell, hands steady now from adrenaline and focus.

The Santa Fe police answered, and Caldwell found his way to an officer who knew who he was. "We're on the main road heading to the reservation side exit. Lou Dawg is tied up in his trailer. It's at the end of the road. Bring security. Bring guns. Bring people with teeth."

The reply was quick, the kind of clipped, efficient answer Caldwell liked: We're on it. Don't stop until you're in Santa Fe.

Holly's shoulder dropped fractionally. Caldwell let himself exhale as they passed the area where the Ford was parked, turned out of the reservation, and onto the highway. The road ahead was still long and dangerous, but the phone in their hands was a thread back to leverage. People they hoped would move without blinking at GulfTex's money.

They kept driving. The mesa fell away in the rearview. Behind them, under the shallow darkness of the reservation, a man was bound and furious and holiday lights blinked like a cruel joke.

Santa's truck rolled in the distance, headlights a pair of slow, steady eyes. It hugged the center line, moving toward the reservation's entrance. Unbeknownst to both, the two vehicles had missed passing each other by minutes.

For now, the highway carried them out of immediate danger. But Caldwell knew the highway didn't so much separate them from what had happened as put them on the path where the next part of the fight would begin. It was a long drive back to Santa Fe.

CHAPTER ELEVEN

The trailer door banged open and stopped, caught by its chain. Santa stepped inside, boots heavy on the warped floor. His eyes slid over the dim, empty space until they landed on Lou Dawg, trussed to a chair, tape across his mouth, sweat streaking his face.

For a long beat, Santa didn't move. He just stood there, knife already in hand. He switched it open, the blade catching a dull gleam from the light.

A heavy parka, black and padded against the desert cold, stretched over his broad shoulders. His beard was salt-and-pepper, trimmed neat, but thick enough to give him a rough, wintry look that explained the nickname. His eyes were pale and hard, glinting like ice under the brim of a knit cap pulled low.

He moved with quiet efficiency, no wasted effort. The air seemed to grow colder in the cramped space.

Lou Dawg saw the knife and stiffened. His chest rose and fell, fast, his eyes narrowing. He stared at the blade.

Santa closed the distance—slow, deliberate, sinister. Lou

Dawg leaned back hard in the chair, the wood creaking under his weight. The knife lifted, poised above him.

Then, with a quick flick, Santa sliced the rope. Lou Dawg's arms snapped free. He tore the tape from his mouth with a snarl, relieved he wasn't bleeding out.

"Dammit, Santa. Took you long enough. They got the upper hand then tied me up."

Santa's voice was flat, cold. "Those two played you for a fool, that's all."

"They took my phone. Caldwell's packing my rifle." Lou Dawg rubbed at the rope burns, fury in his eyes. "I'll kill him."

Santa retracted the knife, slid it in his pocket, and jerked his head toward the door. "Not if I do first. Let's move."

Santa straightened, towering in the small space, and for a moment the trailer felt like a cage, one Lou Dawg was lucky to be let out of.

Chico, who had been watching the men from under the sofa, ran into the bedroom and hid under the bed. When the two men went outside, he did not follow.

Santa climbed inside and his truck growled to life, headlights throwing long knives of light across the scrub and dirt. Lou Dawg climbed in beside him, silent now, shame burning hotter than his anger. They sped to the reservation's exit, gravel spraying in their wake.

Parked nearby was Lou Dawg's Ford pickup, waiting like a ghost from another fight. Santa braked hard.

"This is where we split," Santa said.

Lou Dawg slid out, boots crunching on the gravel. He glanced at Santa, still half expecting the knife to flash. But Santa only reached back to the gun rack and grabbed a shotgun. As Lou Dawg checked his pockets for his keys, Santa propped the shotgun against his thigh.

Then Lou Dawg remembered. "They took my keys; I'll have to hotwire it."

What an idiot, thought Santa.

"Which way?" Lou Dawg asked.

Santa stared down the blacktop, jaw tight. "That's the problem. We don't know." He pointed. "They're bound to head toward a town with police. You take north. I'll take south. One of us will run them down."

Lou Dawg's grin was jagged. "And when I do—"

Santa cut him off. "Call me if you get to them first and don't screw it up again."

"They took my phone."

Showing exasperation, Santa reached in the glove box, took out one of four burners and tossed it to Lou Dawg. "If I find them first, you can turn around and head my way. Same for me if you find them first."

Lou Dawg walked toward the Ford. Santa took off without waiting to see if he got the truck started.

"Thanks a lot," Lou Dawg said to the receding taillights.

Lou Dawg jerked the wires out from under the dash and sparked the truck to life, then roared off in the opposite direction, engine splitting the night. One north toward Santa Fe, one south toward Albuquerque. Somewhere ahead, Caldwell and Holly's SUV carried them closer to safety, or straight into a trap.

The SUV ate up the blacktop, headlights carving a narrow path through the desert night. Holly's fingers were locked around the steering wheel, knuckles bone-white. Caldwell sat twisted in the passenger seat, rifle braced across his lap, scanning the rearview for shadows. They had plenty of gas, but the small engine did not have a lot of go power.

He looked at Lou Dawg's phone. "We need to stay off the line; we've got very little battery left."

"It's okay. The police should be headed toward us." Holly hoped.

For a while, the road was empty. Just the hum of tires and the whisper of wind across the mesa. Holly allowed herself one shaky breath.

Then Caldwell's head snapped to the mirror. "Lights."

Two high beams appeared behind them out of nowhere, barreling fast.

Holly's stomach dropped as she tried to identify the vehicle. It was not friendly.

The truck closed in, grill filling the mirror like a set of jaws. Holly floored it, but the SUV barely increased in speed. Lou Dawg laid on the horn—a long, furious blast, and then slammed into their bumper. The SUV jolted, metal shrieking, Holly fighting the wheel. Caldwell raised the rifle.

"Hold steady!" Caldwell barked. He leaned out his window, rifle in hand, searching for a shot.

The truck hit them again, harder. The SUV fishtailed, tires screaming on asphalt. Holly clenched her jaw, fought the skid, brought them back in line.

Lou Dawg laughed behind the glass, wild-eyed, riding their bumper like a predator teasing its prey. He swerved left, right, clipping the SUV's flank, sparks flying where steel kissed steel. Holly was in the wrong lane. She prayed for no oncoming traffic.

Lou Dawg moved into the other lane trying to pull up beside them.

"Brake!" Caldwell shouted.

Holly slammed the pedal. The SUV lurched, Lou Dawg's truck shooting past. He overcorrected, fishtailing before recovering.

Caldwell shot and hit the back window, but not Lou Dawg. Glass flew.

Holly jammed the accelerator, lurching forward. They passed him but the truck was built for the road. Lou Dawg gunned it, ramming their side, trying to force them into the ditch. Sinister.

The world became chaos, horn blaring, tires squealing, rifle clutched tight as the SUV bucked under the assault. Holly's breath came fast, ragged.

Lou Dawg lost speed but caught up. When the truck came at them again, Holly screamed.

Caldwell growled. His eyes locked on the empty stretch of highway ahead. "Hang on."

Lou Dawg swung left, matching their speed, pressing harder. The road narrowed, shoulder dropping into a dry wash. Holly's arms trembled as she fought the wheel, her whole body locked against the crushing force.

Caldwell twisted, raised the rifle. His finger found the trigger.

The truck surged again, metal grinding, sparks flying until Caldwell squeezed off a shot.

The blast cracked through the night. Lou Dawg's windshield spider-webbed. The truck wavered, swerved, slowed, but didn't stop.

Lou Dawg howled, doubled down, caught up, and slammed into them one more time.

The SUV tipped, swaying on the edge of the shoulder, tires clawing for grip. Holly screamed again, fighting the pull of gravity as Lou Dawg bore down again, relentless.

The SUV screamed down the highway, Holly gripping the wheel so hard her arms ached. Lou Dawg's Ford clung to their side, smashing against them in bursts of grinding metal. Caldwell leaned half out the passenger window, rifle braced, eyes narrowed against the rush of desert wind.

When Caldwell shot at the Ford, Lou Dawg dropped back behind the SUV and swerved left and then right, creating a moving target. As Caldwell tried to steady the rifle to shoot, a second truck, a heavy Dodge, roared up beside them. It was massive and menacing, its engine a deep-throated growl. As it straightened out, Holly saw a lone man inside. Then Holly's breath hitched.

"Oh God," she whispered. "Must be Santa."

Caldwell saw it too. His gut clenched. "Lou Dawg must have alerted him."

Santa gunned the Dodge, headlights flooding the highway. In the mirror, Lou Dawg whooped and swung wide on the shoulder on the passenger side, the two trucks boxing the SUV in like wolves circling prey. They weren't only being chased anymore, they were trapped.

Holly threaded the wheel left and right, desperate to keep the SUV between the two overpowering mechanical forces. Tires screamed as all three vehicles wove across the two-lane strip, engines bellowing in a violent chorus.

"Keep it straight!" Caldwell shouted over the chaos. He braced the rifle on the door, sighted, and squeezed the trigger.

The shot cracked. Lou Dawg's front tire exploded in a shower of rubber. His truck swerved hard, sparks shrieking as the bare rim tore into the asphalt.

The Ford fell back as it fishtailed, skidding across both lanes, showers of fire spitting into the night. Holly tried to put distance between them, knuckles slippery on the wheel.

For a heartbeat, it looked like he'd lose it. But Lou Dawg

came back with a vengeance, grinning behind the shattered glass. Rim grinding, the truck clawed back onto the road, throwing a comet's tail of sparks as he bore down again.

"He's not stopping!" Holly cried.

At the same time, Santa's Dodge slammed sideways, jolting the SUV. The three vehicles ground together in a storm of steel and light, the smell of burning rubber choking the air.

When Santa fell back, Caldwell fired blind out the back window, the blast deafening inside the SUV. The round punched through Santa's grille, but the Dodge didn't falter. It surged closer, herding them into Lou Dawg's sparking death-machine as it pulled up to the SUV again.

Holly screamed, wrenched the wheel, and the SUV shot between the two trucks, missing steel by inches.

Holly saw the faint glow of Santa Fe trembling on the horizon.

"We're almost there."

A steady snow began to fall, blurring her view and adding to the danger at high speeds.

Caldwell still leaned out the window, rifle braced, eyes locked on the nightmare unfolding in their mirrors. Santa's Dodge alternating from behind, then beside them, Lou Dawg's Ford grinding alongside, sparks flying.

They crested a rise and the headlights revealed a narrow bridge spanning a dry gulch, guardrails glinting like thin bones in the dark.

"Hold it steady," Caldwell shouted. "Keep it off the guardrails."

Holly's foot stayed flat on the accelerator. They shot onto the bridge, the SUV shuddering over the joints in the pavement. Behind them, Lou Dawg tried to squeeze past. Santa surged up too, his Dodge snarling.

All three vehicles collided in a cacophony of shrieking metal. The Ford clipped the SUV, bounced off, then slammed sideways into the bridge, and the tangle of steel crunched against the guardrail. The bridge shuddered.

Lou Dawg's truck lurched, half over the edge. His face flashed wild in the dim cab light as his front axle gave way. The Ford toppled, plunging into the gulch. His scream was swallowed by the night before the crash echoed up from below.

Santa rammed them toward the rail. Holly gasped. The SUV skidded sideways, wheels perched on the edge, the guardrail buckling beneath their weight. She and Caldwell lost consciousness as the airbags inflated.

When Caldwell awoke, the SUV was hanging over the side with Santa's Dodge pressed against it from above. It began to sway as Caldwell shook his head and looked for Holly. He unfastened both of their seatbelts and pulled her toward the passenger door which was hanging off the side of the SUV. She roused as he moved her, then shrieked as she saw the distance to the ground below.

"We have to get out!" Caldwell bellowed. He looked for the rifle but had no time to find it. He grabbed Holly's waist and pushed her out and up the side of the SUV. She clawed her way up the sagging vehicle on to the bridge deck. When she was clear, Caldwell followed her up, the SUV teetering with his weight. They embraced on the bridge as the SUV groaned beside them, then broke loose. It toppled, slowly at first, then faster, until it vanished over the side, joining Lou Dawg's Ford in a heap of metal.

Santa's Dodge, having been caught in the crush, and held by the SUV, released and teetered on the rail, truck bed hanging out over the gulch. Its engine growled weakly, head-lights painting empty air as the vehicle swung from side to side.

Caldwell and Holly staggered forward. They peered through the window. Santa slumped in the driver's seat, face bloodied, chest heaving. He turned his head, lips curling in a half smile, half snarl.

The distant keening of sirens broke up the night like a knife. At first it was a thread, one thin wail far down the black ribbon of highway, then it swelled, closer, urgent. Holly froze, the sound cutting clean through the aftershock of metal and the hiss of cooling engines.

The Dodge trembled on the rail, its grille bent, one head-light flickered and died. Santa moved in the driver's seat, blood matted at his temple, breath shallow and ragged. He looked up as the sirens rose and something like recognition crossed his face. Not surprise, but the satisfaction of a man who'd counted on chaos to cover him and was sure it would again.

"This isn't over," he rasped and reached a bloody hand toward the window.

Caldwell's first reflex was relief at the arrival of the police. Backup. Authority. A last, lawful hand to put the night to bed. But the relief curdled fast. He thought of Holly, of how small and raw she'd been a few hours ago.

Across from him, Holly's jaw worked. Her breath came shallow. The sirens drew nearer, a steady thread that would bring uniforms, questions. Neighbors. Reporters. Lawyers. Men with ties who bought silence for the right price.

Would they—could they—ever be safe?

Caldwell felt the world narrow to the metal rail near his feet and the warm, shallow life in Santa's chest. If the police found Santa alive on this bridge, bleeding, with his truck teetering over a gulch, the story would spin in directions they could not control. Santa would open his mouth. He'd work his bullshit. GulfTex would use their endless supply of money.

Holly's face flinched at the thought.

"Caldwell?" she breathed. There was no accusation in it. Just a raw, terrible question.

He looked at her, really looked at the blood at her temple, the dust in her hair, the way her hands trembled. The sirens screamed closer, imminently present, lights beginning to wash the highway in blue and white.

They had minutes. Maybe less.

Holly's eyes flashed. For a fraction of a second, she looked like someone who had decided to stop being afraid. Her eyes said what she could not. *Let's finish it.*

They moved together in a single motion, two people who'd been dragged through the same storm and chose the same brutal harbor. Caldwell shoved against the Dodge's front bumper with both hands as Holly planted her boots and threw her weight behind him. The truck rocked, a slow, shuddering protest. Santa's moan turned to a curse as he saw them through the windshield. He dragged a hand up as if to rise, their intentions becoming clear.

The Dodge slithered a fraction, then another. The edge of the guardrail cracked under the combined weight and force. Holly's shoulder slammed into Caldwell's back. The truck leaned, then tipped.

Time stretched. The Dodge pitched, upended, and broke the rail. It fell in a slow, catastrophic arc and slammed into the wreckage below where Lou Dawg's Ford and the rented SUV were still smoldering. Steel met steel in a final, violent punctuation, fuel hissed, and then flames took hold with immediate, ravenous hunger.

Caldwell jerked Holly backward as heat licked the undersides of the bridge. The patrol cars skidded to a halt, blue lights swallowing the deck. Officers poured out, shouting, their flashlights cutting through smoke and dust.

Holly's breath hitched as she pressed her forehead to Caldwell's shoulder. He held her, chest tight with something halfway between relief and anger that had no time to form. The flames below screamed up, swallowing twisted metal, consuming the three trucks in a furnace that removed everything. Gone was the evidence, the men, the proof, and left behind was only heat and ash.

Caldwell straightened slowly, met Holly's eyes. There were questions coming that would not be answered by silence. There were decisions to be lived with for the rest of their lives. Both were fine with that.

CHAPTER TWELVE

The night sky flickered orange and red behind them, smoke curling from the canyon where the three vehicles had gone up in flames. Sirens swelled until the patrol cars slid to a stop across the bridge, blue and red lights splashing across Caldwell and Holly. Officers fanned out with pistols raised, shouting commands.

Caldwell lifted his hands and encouraged Holly to do the same. They were hustled toward the nearest cruiser. The acrid taste of gasoline hung in the air.

Detective Sampson recognized Caldwell and motioned to the officers not to cuff them.

Caldwell introduced Holly. "This is my fiancée. She was kidnapped and held against her will."

"I'm so glad you're both safe. I'll take your statements at the police station." He looked at them both and the results of the airbag deployment. "We'll get you some medical care."

Inside the squad car, with the plexiglass between them and the uniforms up front, Caldwell leaned close to Holly. His voice was low, urgent, almost drowned by the crackle of radios.

"Let me be a lawyer for a minute," he said. His eyes bored into hers, steadying her. She nodded her consent.

"When we get downtown, they'll want to separate us. Interrogate us. If they try to push you about anything beyond the kidnapping, you play it vague. Act disoriented. Say you need a doctor. Say your head's swimming, you can't remember details other than being forced off the road, the airbag inflating, that type of thing."

Holly swallowed, her hands trembling in her lap. "What if they press me about the chase? About what we did?"

"The chase was so fast, it's a blur. You don't remember anything after the collision on the bridge. The airbags deflated, and that's your last recollection," Caldwell said, sharper now. "You were terrified, shoved around, blacked out. Stick to that. Keep the focus on being kidnapped. That's enough truth to hold up. Everything else never happened."

She glanced toward the windshield where smoke still smudged the horizon. Her chin quivered, but she gave a quick nod. "Okay. Medical help. Don't remember. Confused. Nothing more."

"That's right," Caldwell said, settling back against the vinyl seat as the squad car lurched forward. He forced himself to exhale. "Let me handle the rest."

The cruiser pulled away from the bridge, its headlights cutting a path through the desert dark. Behind them, the flames died down without confession.

The glass doors of the Santa Fe police station sighed open, spilling them into a lobby humming with late-night activity. Uniformed officers exchanged quick looks at two people fresh off a nightmare, bleeding, clothes torn, soot on their faces. An officer gestured toward a corridor.

"This way. We'll need to ask you both some questions."

Caldwell guided Holly close at his side. The skin burns where she'd been tied were red and bleeding in places. Her face was swollen and red. She was trembling in the big jacket, though she held her chin high. When they reached the fork in the hallway, two detectives waited, Sampson and a gray-haired woman. The female pointed to the left. "I'm Detective Marquez." Then to Holly, "Miss, we'll talk to you in here. Mr. Beck, you'll go with Detective Sampson."

Caldwell froze, tightening his arm around Holly. "No. We stay together."

"Sir, it's standard procedure," the female detective said, already opening the door. "We need to get your statements separately."

"Not tonight," Caldwell snapped. His voice carried down the hall, sharp enough to stop a passing officer. "She was kidnapped. Terrified. I'm not leaving her side while she's barely holding it together. She needs a doctor."

"Mr. Beck."

"You want her statement? You get it with me in the room," Caldwell said, steel in his tone. "Otherwise, you'll have a victim collapsing on the floor before you get two sentences. That's not good police work."

Holly gripped his sleeve like it was a lifeline. "Please. I need him with me."

Detective Marquez glanced at Detective Sampson, who nodded.

"All right." Her voice was calm. "We'll bend protocol. You two can stay together, as long as you both cooperate."

Caldwell let out a slow breath and nodded. "We'll cooperate. But together."

Minutes later, they sat in a small room with a single table, the air sharp with disinfectant and the faint hum of fluorescent lights. Holly still clutched Caldwell's hand beneath the table, her knuckles white, as if letting go meant she might vanish again. A uniformed officer brought them hot coffee and cold ice packs.

Detectives Sampson and Marquez opened their respective notebooks, pens poised. "Okay. Start from the beginning," Sampson said gently. "Tell me what these people wanted and how this all led to that bridge tonight."

Caldwell leaned forward. He spoke evenly, his eyes never leaving hers.

"You already know about the initial kidnapping. It started when we rented the Airbnb in Santa Fe for the holidays. I went out, just to Whole Foods, on a grocery run. When I came back, the place was disturbed. Holly was gone."

"Yes, that part we know. Continue."

Holly squeezed his hand under the table. He steadied her with a glance, then went on.

"I didn't know it then, but GulfTex Holdings had decided to make me their problem and their unwilling partner. I represent a land owner named Louis Johnson in a litigation case against GulfTex. His oil and gas reserves are worth millions, maybe billions. My motion in court could have shut down their development plans. It would have prohibited them from continuing the court action if we got a motion for summary judgment to dismiss the lawsuit."

Detective Marquez asked, "Would that just be a temporary help to them?"

Caldwell nodded. "I assume they wanted it to go to trial so they could work it all the way up to the appellate court, if necessary. They are very plugged in at high levels. So instead of fighting it legally, they went off the books. They hired a fixer who called himself Santa. He subcontracted the dirty work to a thug named Lou Dawg who lived out on the Cochiti Reservation. Those were their trucks that burned up with our SUV."

Detective Sampson's brow furrowed, but he kept his pen moving.

"Santa made it clear that if I sabotaged my own client's case, if I withdrew the motion and missed the deadline, Holly would be returned. If I didn't, she'd disappear forever. Lou Dawg was the one who broke into Casa Pequeno and dragged her out. Later, he cut and delivered a lock of her hair in a package left on the doorstep."

Holly shuddered.

Caldwell squeezed her hand tighter. "It terrified me. From there, it was continued threats, coercion, intimidation."

Detective Marquez let out a long breath. "How did you find out where she was?"

"I figured out what Holly meant by *blue glass*, by going through the photos on her phone. When I made my way to the reservation to find the artist, little did I know that Lou Dawg was following me. If he hadn't, I probably would not have found Holly. It was a blessing in disguise. I may have never located his trailer as the artist, his mother, is now deceased and didn't share that address."

Marquez wrote a note. "So, they caught you on the highway trying to escape?"

"A lot happened after we got the upper hand with Lou Dawg. We left him tied up in the trailer, but Santa must have found him and cut him loose. The rest is all about trying to outrun them back to Santa Fe, all leading to the chase on the bridge."

"Go on." Sampson was getting the picture. "Before you left

the reservation, why didn't you go to the Tribal Police or to a house on the reservation?"

"We had no idea where the Tribal Police were located, and we never passed another house once we turned onto the reservation and drove to the trailer. We didn't know if anyone else was in on it. We just wanted to get back here to you. That's why we called. We thought we were out ahead of them and could get back to Santa Fe before they caught us. We were wrong."

The detective finally set the pen down. "And those two men, Santa and Lou Dawg? How did they wind up in that gulch?"

"They lost control of their own plan," Caldwell said carefully. "You've seen the wreckage. They came after us and we barely climbed out. They weren't so lucky."

The detective leaned back, arms crossed, weighing Caldwell. Then, he looked at Holly.

Caldwell pressed on. "Detective, you can see why it's critical that I get to a computer. The GulfTex motion has to be handled tonight. I need to secure filings, put evidence in the record, and protect my client's case."

The detective studied him for a long moment, wondering if Caldwell had gotten lucky or whether he'd helped engineer the demise of Santa and Lou Dawg. Then he rose from his chair, gesturing toward the door.

"All right, Mr. Beck. Come with me. We'll get you to a computer."

CHAPTER THIRTEEN

The station had quieted to a low hum. Most of the chaos from the night was gone, just a dispatcher's voice on the radio, the smell of coffee from somewhere down the hall, the occasional cough from a patrolman finishing his shift. Outside, the desert sky had slipped into the sweet stillness of the small morning light.

Caldwell now sat in front of a government-issue desktop computer, its monitor buzzing faintly under the harsh fluorescent lights. Holly dozed on a padded bench along the wall, wrapped in a gray blanket given to her by an EMT, the huge jacket discarded, her head tilted to one side. She looked worn out but safe, and that gave Caldwell the strength to push through the exhaustion pulling at his own bones. He straightened in the chair, cracked his knuckles, and pulled the keyboard closer.

The familiar login page for the Harris County Courts filled the screen. His pulse kicked up as he typed in his credentials. After a beat too long, the screen changed to ACCESS GRANTED.

He navigated his way through the site until the case docket appeared: *Johnson v. GulfTex Holdings*. The motion he'd set up to be filed before he left Houston, the Motion to Dismiss was there, grayed out, tagged READY TO FILE. He remembered hitting that button, his stomach twisted in knots, Santa's ultimatum replaying in his head. He'd almost sold out his client to save Holly's life. He'd do it again.

Not anymore. His finger hovered for a beat. Once he clicked, it would be public record. GulfTex's attorneys would see it first thing when they logged in. The fuse would be relit. Who knew what they'd do next, but this crisis was averted.

Caldwell clicked to file the motion. The document loaded slowly, the system dragging like it knew the stakes. Finally, the notification appeared: FILED.

He glanced over his shoulder at Holly. She stirred in her sleep, murmured something, then settled again. That was all he needed.

Caldwell turned back and double-checked the filing and sent the confirmation to the printer down the hall and to his email.

Next, he waited the half hour until business hours, picked up the phone, and called his law firm in Houston.

As he finished a long explanation with his partners, Holly stirred on the sofa, the gray blanket slipping from her shoulders. She blinked against the glare and stretched her aching muscles.

Across the room, Caldwell was on the phone. His free hand raked through his hair as he listened, then he said something sharp and final before hanging up.

When he turned, his eyes found hers immediately. Relief flickered there.

"You're awake," he said softly, crossing to her.

"What was that?" Holly pushed the blanket aside and sat up straighter. "Who were you talking to?"

"My partners," Caldwell said, lowering himself to sit beside her. His voice was steady but edged with fatigue. "I didn't get a chance to tell you during the chase, but Bob Dwyer was in on it. He admitted it when I called him from the rental. That's how they knew that we were in Santa Fe."

Holly's face hardened, her hand tightening on the arm of the chair. "Dwyer? The kid you trained?"

He nodded once. "Yeah. I told the partners everything just now. They're furious, and they're moving fast. They'll coordinate with Houston PD. He'll be arrested before noon."

Holly exhaled, a shaky sound that was half laugh, half sigh. "So, it wasn't just them out there. It was inside your own house."

"Right in the middle of it," Caldwell muttered. His jaw flexed, a muscle ticking. "But it's over for him now."

She reached across, fingers curling around his hand. "Then let's be done with him too. No more ghosts. No more traitors."

Caldwell squeezed back, the faintest flicker of resolve rising through his exhaustion. For the first time since the nightmare began, he let himself believe it was finished. He looked at the clock on the wall. The courthouse would be open by now, and GulfTex would be waiting and watching. For the first time in days, he felt like he'd drawn blood on the right side of the battlefield.

"It's done. Let's get out of here. I'll tell Detective Sampson we're ready to go."

The next day, morning light spilled through the thin curtains of Casa Pequeno. They had slept in until the last possible moment before check out. The place was quiet now, stripped of the terror it had held only nights before, but Caldwell still felt the echo of it in the walls.

Holly moved slowly through the bedroom, wincing only occasionally as she folded clothes into her suitcase. He watched her for a moment. Her movements were steady, methodical. It was the look of someone forcing order on chaos.

"Almost done?" he asked, zipping his own bag shut.

"Just about," she said, pausing to press a sweater to her chest before laying it flat. "I'll be glad to get out of here. Santa Fe's beautiful, but..." Her voice trailed off.

"But this trip's over," Caldwell finished for her. "Houston will feel good. Just in time for Christmas."

She smiled faintly, but her eyes stayed shadowed.

The ringtone startled them both. Caldwell fished his phone from his pocket. Caller ID: Santa Fe Police.

He answered. "Detective?"

Sampson's voice was deep, steady, with a faint rasp. "Mr. Beck, I wanted you to hear this straight from me. Early this morning, we coordinated with Federal authorities. The head of GulfTex operations was taken into custody."

Caldwell straightened, catching Holly's gaze. "They got him?" He switched the call to speaker so Holly could hear.

"That's right," Sampson confirmed. "But here's the thing, it's out of our hands now. The Santa Fe police are officially off the case. The Feds are taking over. FBI, DOJ, maybe both. Prosecution's a different ballgame and they'll be the ones running it."

Caldwell's jaw tightened. "So where does that leave us?"

"I've already given them your contact information," Sampson said. "You and Miss Rowe should expect to hear from Federal agents soon. They'll want statements. You're on their radar now."

They both let out a slow breath.

The detective continued. "I wanted you both to hear it from me, before it comes down the pipeline. A national news anchor named Ernest Anguish has picked up the story. There may be press sniffing around."

Caldwell and Holly shared eye contact. The last thing they needed was scrutiny and questions.

"You did good here, Beck. You went above and beyond. I'm just sorry we didn't help you more. We would have if we could have. I did send a copy of our report to your car rental company, so at least you won't be dinged for that."

Caldwell was quiet, his hand tightening around the phone. Holly leaned close, listening. If only they'd helped him when he first went to the station things may have turned out differently.

"Thank you, Detective," Caldwell said finally.

"You two take care of yourselves," Sampson replied. "Safe travels home."

The line clicked dead.

Caldwell slipped the phone back into his pocket and looked at Holly.

Holly's lips pressed into a thin line. "Guess we can't just walk away from this, can we?"

Caldwell zipped her suitcase shut and pulled it upright. "No. But at least now it's in the right hands. And we'll be ready when they call."

They exchanged a long look, the weight of everything unspoken between them. Then Caldwell reached for the handle of her bag. "Come on. Let's go home."

The red replacement SUV rolled slowly through the narrow streets of Santa Fe, tires crunching over a thin crust of snow that had just begun to fall. Rooftops were dusted white, chili pepper lights still twinkled from balconies and doorframes, the town wearing its holiday charm like nothing dark had ever touched it.

Caldwell drove with one hand on the wheel, the other resting on Holly's knee. Neither spoke for a while; the hum of the heater and the faint hiss of the tires filled the quiet. At the edge of town, as the road opened to the highway toward Albuquerque Airport, Caldwell finally broke the silence.

"You know," he said, his voice low but certain, "I thought I'd lost you. More than once. And I realized something."

Holly turned her head toward him, her eyes shining. "What's that?"

"That I don't want to waste another day doubting what we have. Or whether it's worth fighting for."

He slowed, easing the SUV on to the shoulder. Snowflakes spun in the headlights like silver sparks. From his coat pocket, he pulled out the ring he hadn't been able to bear looking at the past days. He reached for her hand.

Her breath caught as he slid the engagement ring back onto her finger, the diamond catching the glow of the dashboard lights.

"It belongs here," Caldwell said simply. "With you. Always."

Holly's throat worked as tears welled. She looked at the ring, then back at him, her smile breaking through. "I love you, Caldwell. More than I can ever say. I'm sorry I ever took it off."

He leaned over, kissed her, the world outside dissolving into snow and silence. When he settled back, Holly put her hand on his thigh. With her other hand, she reached for the radio, twisting the dial. Static gave way to a familiar swell of strings and Bing Crosby's voice, warm and nostalgic.

I'm dreaming of a white Christmas...

Holly turned it up, laughing through her tears, and held her hand up to admire the ring once more, the diamond gleaming against the falling snow beyond the windshield.

Caldwell put the SUV back in gear and guided them on to the highway, heading south the same way they'd come in. The snow thickened, wrapping the desert in white. And for the first time in a long time, they both felt ready to go home.

THE END

BULLET BOOKS

SPEED READS

ON A PLANE...ON A TRAIN...FASTER THAN A SPEEDING BULLET

BULLET BOOKS are speed reads for the busy traveler, commuter, or beach-goer. All are new original crime fiction stories that can be read in two to three hours. Gripping cinematic mysteries and thrillers by your favorite authors!

Page turners for fans who want to escape into a good read.

ALL ABOARD!

www.bulletbooksspeedreads.com

#1 Sinister Santa
#2 Iron 13
#3 Bloody Bead
#4 The Hot Seat
#5 Stabbed
#6 Man in the Client Chair
#7 Only a Pawn in Their Game
#8 Dangerous Practice
#9 Two Bodies One Grave
#10 Last Call
#11 The Last Straw
#12 The Neon Palm
#13 Loser's Gumbo

LEAVE A REVIEW

If you enjoyed this book, please leave a REVIEW on Amazon or Goodreads. Reviews are the lifeblood of authors and often determine whether other readers purchase books when they shop. Thank you.

Keep up with the latest

books and giveaways here:

www.bulletbooksspeedreads.com

www.starpathbooks.com

www.facebook.com/bulletbooksspeedreads/

Bill Rodgers

In addition to publishing short form humor, Bill Rodgers writes action-filled thrillers with an element of mystery. Bill has written for Jay Leno for over twenty years, and his material has been used in Jay's monologues and comedy routines around the world. Bill's writing has taken many forms, including sitcom scripts, stage plays, and action-comedy screenplays.

www.bill-rodgers.com

Manning Wolfe

Manning Wolfe, an award-winning author and attorney residing in Austin, Texas, writes cinematic-style, fast-paced crime fiction. Her legal thriller series features Austin Lawyer Merit Bridges. Manning is co-author of the popular Bullet Books Speed Reads, a series of crime fiction books for readers on the go. As a graduate of Rice University and the University of Texas School of Law, Manning's experience has given her a voyeur's peek into some shady characters' lives and a front row seat to watch the good people who stand against them.

www.manningwolfe.com

Starpath Books, LLC

Austin, Texas

www.starpathbooks.com

Bullet Books Speed Reads and Starpath Books, LLC provide authors for speaking events such as book clubs, book signings and library presentations. To find out more, go to www.starpathbooks.com or email: media@starpathbooks.com.

ISBN EBook: 978-1-944225-58-2

ISBN Paperback: 978-1-944225-59-9

10 9 8 7 6 5 4 3 2 1

Printed in the United States of America